Elena Kincaid, Maia Dylan, and Sarah Marsh

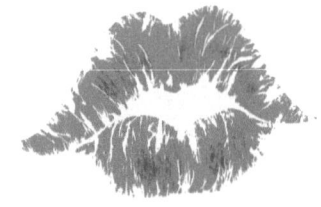

EVERNIGHT PUBLISHING ®

www.evernightpublishing.com

Copyright© 2017

Elena Kincaid, Maia Dylan, and Sarah Marsh

Editor: Karyn White

Cover Artist: Jay Aheer

ISBN: 978-1-77339-371-1

Elena Kincaid, Maia Dylan, and Sarah Marsh

DEDICATION

We would like to dedicate this book in loving memory of our good friend, John Tucker. He was a friend, supporter, mentor, and a wonderful man. He will be deeply missed.

Don't cry because it's over, smile because it happened.

—Dr. Seuss

Elena Kincaid, Maia Dylan, and Sarah Marsh

DECIDING HER FAETE

Beyond the Veil, 2

Elena Kincaid, Maia Dylan, and Sarah Marsh

Copyright © 2016

Prologue

That light! What the hell is that light?

"What did you do to him?" Mrs. Nieves yelled at April.

"N-nothing," she stuttered. "He fell. I told him not to climb on the counter, but he didn't listen and then he fell." She couldn't get to him in time to catch him.

"Get away from him," she yelled again. Mrs. Nieves looked genuinely scared of her. "You're the devil's child." She cradled Michael in her arms, surprisingly uncaring of the blood currently staining her new pink cashmere sweater. "They saddled me with a red-headed devil."

"I am not," April shouted back. She knew Mrs. Nieves didn't like her. April was just a paycheck to her, as were her other three foster kids, but she did nothing wrong. She had told him not to climb and she was only trying to help him when he fell, but there was so much blood.

April wept as she looked down at her bloodstained hands and then back down at Michael, who lay still in the cold woman's arms. She'd never get out of her head the sound of his head thumping hard on the kitchen tiles. And she could have sworn she saw a white and blue light flickering in the palms of her hands. She'd seen it many times before in her dreams, only this time, this definitely wasn't a dream.

"They'll never give me any more kids," Mrs. Nieves cried. "They'll blame me for this for sure," she said shrilly, looking up at April.

"Is that all he is to you, bitch? A paycheck? We need to call 911. He needs help." April had had enough. A ten-year-old boy lay bleeding in her arms, and all the heartless shrew could worry about was money. "If you fed us enough, if you used that money for groceries for the kids you're responsible for like you're *supposed* to, he wouldn't have needed to climb up and hunt for food."

"Don't you dare speak to me like that, you little devil. I saw that voodoo shit you were trying to do."

"I don't know what you're talk—"

"Always knew there was something strange about you," Mrs. Nieves cut her off, her face a cruel mask. April could almost see the wheels turning in her head as an idea was forming. "They are not pinning this one on me."

April balled her hands into fists, and a murderous rage the likes of which she had never experienced encompassed her. She flew at Mrs. Nieves, knocking her down, separating her from Michael.

"It's *your* fault he's hurt," April spat as she cradled Michael in her arms. April had never been more grateful that the two younger kids, a brother and sister, were not at home to witness this. Their birth mother had been fighting to regain custody of them, so Mr. Nieves had taken them to court.

The cold woman lifted her head, and her eyes went wide with fear. April thought that Mrs. Nieves feared being hit again, but when April looked down at her own hands, she saw the real reason behind her sheer terror. As she held onto Michael, the same white and blue lights dimly emitted from her palms.

And then Michael opened up his eyes.

Elena Kincaid, Maia Dylan, and Sarah Marsh

Chapter One

"April? Earth to April."

"What?" She looked up to see her coworker, Dee, staring expectantly at her.

"I asked if you were in or not." Dee huffed impatiently. "A bunch of us are going to Wave for some drinks after work." Then she added, "Where do you go when you do that thing you do?"

"What thing?"

"Your spacing out thing. You've been doing it more than usual lately."

Dee was right, of course. Her nightmares had become even more frequent as of late and dredging up old memories she definitely did not want to revisit. Like the incident with Michael. No one believed Mrs. Nieves and her crazy ramblings about April's so-called voodoo, not even April herself. Michael must not have hit his head as hard as she had thought, and April had also been certain that she was in fact not a devil, nor his spawn, nor any kind of witch or voodoo priestess as Mrs. Nieves had claimed her to be.

The light she saw ... well, that she just decided to file away and not drive herself crazy over something she could not understand or explain, something that may have only been imagined in the first place. Besides, other than in her dreams, she had never seen it again.

Something good had managed to come out of Michael's fall. Mrs. Nieves and her husband lost all of their foster children as well as their privilege of ever fostering again. The two younger kids had been returned to their mother, Michael finally got adopted by a nice family, and April, being that she had been nearly sixteen at the time of the incident, had proven herself to be extremely self-sufficient, and got herself emancipated.

The lawyer who had represented April in her emancipation case, Lauren Danvers, a sharp, no-nonsense woman who had two grown daughters of her own, ended up taking April into her home.

April had thought that she would prefer being on her own, as then at least no one would be able to disappoint her anymore, but something about Mrs. Danvers and her family had called to her. After being abandoned at the age of five, with no memory of her past other than her first name, she had bounced around the system and eight different foster homes. At Mrs. Danvers's home, for the first time in April's life, there were no strings attached, no paychecks to be collected. They simply offered her a home and genuinely grew to care for her and her for them. Even after she had made an accidental strange discovery about her pseudo-adoptive family, they didn't kick her out. Instead, they sat her down and opened up a whole new world for her about shifters and other beings which she had once thought fictional.

She had stumbled upon a young boy, maybe a year older than her former foster brother, Michael, in the woods behind the Danvers's house. He lay whimpering in the snow with a gunshot wound in his thigh. "Hunters … they got me this time," he had explained.

April was confused. "Why would they be hunting *you*?"

She discovered the reason when he winced again from the pain and growled low in the back of his throat. Sharp claws extended from his fingernails, and then his eyes glowed before he growled again in a deep animalistic rumble. He should have terrified her, but instead, she found him beautiful. She wanted to take away his pain, put it on herself if she had to.

Without even realizing, she placed her hand on his thigh. "It will be okay," she reassured him. "I'll get you some help."

The boy looked at her with his golden glowing eyes and smiled. "I'm okay now. Thank you."

Once again he confused her. "But I didn't do anything." She took away her bloodied hands and saw that though his thigh still had blood on it, she could no longer see his wound.

She then watched with awed fascination as he changed fully into a brown wolf, larger than any she had ever seen. He gave her cheek a quick swipe with his tongue before running off deeper into the woods.

"I guess we have a lot to talk about," she heard Mrs. Danvers say behind her.

She learned that wolves heal fairly quickly, even from a gunshot wound, but that day in the forest, the injured boy healed at an exceptional rate that saved him from a few hours of pain. She filed that incident away as well. When Mrs. Danvers told her that she had the healing touch, April had found her calling in life. She became a nurse, helping first humans then shifters once she learned their physiology.

She had felt another calling six months ago on her twenty-fourth birthday, one that led her away from her home in Washington State and relocated her to a nursing position at a hospital in Vancouver. That's when the nightmares had started up again and continually progressed in frequency. Images of flashing white and blue lights, screams, and cruel laughter began to haunt her again, but still something in her gut told her she needed to be there in Vancouver.

It had been hard enough to let the Danvers family in emotionally, but making new connections just wasn't her thing. No one could disappoint her if she kept people at bay, so she pretty much had kept to herself and came no closer to figuring out why her gut had drawn her north to work for a human hospital in Canada.

Maybe it was time to change her loner status, she thought. Something inside of her heart had been stirring lately, causing her to feel empty, dead inside. She felt a strong longing that she would not be able to just hide away and compartmentalize. Not this time.

"I'm in," she told Dee. She didn't bother answering Dee's second inquiry. Her memories were her own, and none that she wanted to share with a coworker she barely even knew.

One hour and thirty minutes later and two drinks in, April wished she had just gone straight home. Dee and several coworkers, whose names she couldn't remember, had all paired off and were currently grinding against their possible one night stands. April had done the one night stand thing herself once, and therefore had no room to judge, not that she was the judgmental type in the first place, but she realized from her experience that it did nothing for her. The encounter had only made her feel lonelier, made her yearn for a connection that she feared she would never find. She envied her shifter family and the deep bonds that they formed with their mate or mates.

And April definitely found the sleazy guy with greased up hair sitting next to her severely lacking in the connection department. He also apparently did not understand the meaning of "I am not interested" despite the fact that she had already stated it three times.

"Do you not see what's in my hand?" April held up her gin-and-tonic and jiggled it in front of him, the ice clinking against the glass. "It's called a drink, and I already have one."

"You don't have to keep being such a bitch about it."

"Excuse me?" Now she was mad. *Who the hell does this guy think he is?* "If I am being a bitch, it's because you won't leave me the fuck alone!"

He got in her face then. "That's because I bet you could use a good *fuck*. Then you wouldn't act like such a prudish cunt. Tell me, is the hair on your pussy the same fiery red?"

April shoved him hard away from her before throwing her drink in his face. His expression changed from lascivious to extremely pissed off in an instant. He grabbed her wrist, causing her to whimper from the pain. A moment later, her wrist was free, and she came face to face with a very well defined muscular back, outfitted in a skin tight black t-shirt. His bicep bulged as he twisted the arm of the sleazeball, pinning him to the bar. April tilted her head to the left to see past the man who had come to her rescue, and saw that said sleaze cringed in pain.

"How about I rip out your tongue?" the deep husky voice asked the slimeball. "Then you won't be able to talk that way to a lady again."

The slime's eyes went wide with fear as a few patrons stared at them for a moment, before returning to their drinking and flirting as if this kind of thing happened all the time. Which it probably did, April figured.

"Maybe after that, I'll remove your arms from their sockets so you never place your unwanted hands on a woman."

"Okay, m-man," the sleaze pathetically stammered. "Okay. T-take it easy."

As soon as *sexy back* released him, her greasy

suitor hightailed it out of his seat and disappeared into the crowd.

She had no idea what possessed her to do it, but with his back still to her, probably making sure the asshole didn't try to harm another woman, she couldn't stop from leaning in closer to the tall drink of water and inhaling his scent. His shirt smelled freshly laundered, but it was his woodsy scent that made her mouth water. She felt the sudden urge to lick him, but shook her head to clear her mind of the insane thought. At least she no longer regretted coming out tonight. Things had just gotten a little more interesting.

And then he turned around, and things got *a lot* more interesting. She felt her heart skip a beat as if it forgot how to function properly. She could sense her face redden underneath his penetrating gaze. His sapphire eyes connected with her green ones as if they looked through and inside her. She had the sudden urge to brush away the few strands of dirty blond hair that concealed part of his right eye, because maybe then she'd be able to fully see into the depths of his soul as well.

"Did he hurt you?" the stranger asked with genuine concern. He gently picked up her wrist to examine it, and she immediately pulled it back. It didn't hurt when he touched her, but his touch produced a spark that shot up her entire arm. It scared her.

"I'm sorry," he said. "Let me get you some ice for that."

"No, it's fine." She felt her cheeks redden further. "It doesn't hurt. And thank you … you know, for stepping in when you did."

His brow furrowed, as if in confusion, and then he flexed his hand a few times, the same hand he touched her with, making her wonder if he felt the same spark, too.

"You're welcome." He took the now vacant seat next to her. "What's your name?"

"April."

"I'm Jason." April's eyes went straight to his lips when he told her his name, and she watched as those full lips slowly quirked into a sly smile as he added, "Tell me something, April, do you always like to sniff men who come to your rescue?"

Chapter Two

Jason couldn't hold back his grin as the adorable redhead in front of him blushed furiously at being caught sniffing his back. Sure, he could've just let it go and not said anything, but to a wolf like him, it was the best of compliments that she just couldn't help herself. Truth be told, his own wolf became more than a little excited by her scent as well.

"Umm … oh God! How embarrassing." she laughed along with him as she covered her face with her hand. "No, I normally don't *sniff* strange men."

"Well then," he said moving in a little closer to her, "it seems only fair that I get to do the same, right?"

Her stunning green eyes went wide as he slowly leaned in and lowered his nose toward the warmth of her neck. Jason noticed her hands clenching in her lap. For a moment, he thought she would push him away, but as he lightly ran his nose and lips along her skin under her ear, she let out the barest of moans, and he knew what his wolf had been trying to tell him from the first moment they'd caught her delicate and unusual scent from across the bar. This beautiful woman was his mate.

Now that he got close enough, he tried to figure out what was so unique about her scent, but there was just something he couldn't quite put his finger on. But Gods, she smelled divine.

"You smell good enough to eat, little one," Jason whispered in a low growl before his tongue darted out for a quick taste. He backed up before he lost his control completely.

"Oh!" April gasped as she stared at his face in shock. "You're a wolf."

Jason could only assume that scenting her had brought his wolf closer to the surface, enough that she could see the change in his eyes, but he was also pleasantly surprised that she knew *what* he was. That would save him a lot of explanations.

"You're familiar with my kind?" He knew to tread carefully. "You're not afraid of me, are you?"

"No." She smiled, seemingly amused by his question. "It's odd, but for some reason, I feel like I've known you forever. You must think I'm crazy."

"No, I don't." Jason smiled back, placing his hand over hers. "I think I know exactly how you feel actually. Can I get you another drink?"

"Nah, I think I'm done drinking for tonight." She set her glass on the bar and then looked up at him shyly through her lashes. "But would you maybe want to go grab some food and coffee maybe?"

He found April's fumbling attempt at asking him out extremely adorable, endearing her to him even more. She gave off the impression that she did not ask men out very often, and then his wolf bristled at the idea of his mate spending time with any other male at all … well, any male other than his brother Donovan, of course.

Jason and Donovan had always known they were destined to share the same mate, and he couldn't wait to call his brother and give him the good news. His brother's position in the pack as Beta put a lot of responsibility on Donovan's shoulders, and there were times where Jason would swear he felt his brother's longing for a mate through their bond. They left their previous pack in Alberta when it became obvious that none of the females there belonged to them, and for some reason, after meeting the Vancouver Alpha at the National Summit, they just knew that this city was where they needed to be.

"Yes." Jason smiled back at April. "I'd love that.

We can get a chance to really talk."

"Awesome, just let me go tell my friends that I'm leaving and grab my coat." April jumped off her barstool and moved towards the dance floor. She kept glancing back at him as she moved through the crowd trying to get to a group of people dancing in the center of the dance floor.

Jason knew he only had a few moments, so he quickly texted his brother as he waited for their mate to return.

Jason: **Amazing news. I think I just found our mate, brother, and she's perfect. Her name is April. Going to eat. Will try to get her to come back to the house to meet you.**

He laughed out loud when the only response he got from Donovan was two emoticons—a shocked face and a smiley face. His brother must have been in a meeting if he didn't call back immediately. Jason next texted Ben and Leo, the head Enforcers of their pack, who were most likely at the same meeting. He informed them that he hadn't found any sign of Fae activity at the bar and that he was taking a break at the diner down the street. He switched his phone to silent as April came walking back up to him with her jacket in her arms.

"Ready?" he asked, guiding her toward the door. She nodded with a shy smile.

When they stepped out into the night air, the quiet sound of soft rain was welcoming after the loud music in the club. Jason had thought that he'd get tired of the weather here in Vancouver, as it could change so quickly and rained so often, but surprisingly, he came to appreciate how the water seemed to wash away the hustle and bustle of city life, bringing a calm and soothing feel that most metropolitan areas didn't have. There was nothing more invigorating than the scent of the night air right after the rain had stopped, and Jason loved to shift and run through the woods outside their pack house when the water still clung to the grass.

They left the crowded area in front of the bar and continued down the street as Jason led her to his favorite diner.

"Oh, I love this place," she said looking over at him with a small smile when she noticed where they were headed. "They have the best poutine."

"Ah, I knew we were going to get along famously." He held the door open for her, and briefly shut his eyes as she brushed past him, his skin tingling once again from her touch. Once inside, he offered her the inside of the booth and then slid in next to her. "What could be better than fries, cheese, and gravy?"

"It's because they use real beef gravy that makes it so good," April replied. She dazzled him with a wink. Apparently she dazzled the waitress as well, a middle-aged looking woman who stood waiting to take their order and who must have overheard her comment. The waitress smiled as she jotted down their order, and then returned quickly to drop off two cups of coffee.

"So tell me, April, where are you from?"

"How do you know I'm not from Vancouver?"

"It's the accent." He tapped his ear lightly. "It's very faint, but sounds American to me."

"Wow, you're the first one in the city who's said anything. I didn't really think I had an accent."

"Well, most Canadians from the west don't think we do either," he chuckled, "but apparently we do, too."

"I'm from a small town in Washington, so not too far away."

"And what brought you up north?"

April paused for a moment as if she was thinking

about how to answer. Jason wondered if she was going to lie, or if she had a *reason* to lie about why she relocated.

"To be honest, I don't really know what drew me here. One day I just woke up and felt I was supposed to be somewhere else, so I packed up the car, gave my notice at the hospital, and just started driving." She shrugged and blushed a little when she met his gaze. "Wow, that sounds pretty crazy when I say it out loud."

"Well whatever it was that pulled you here, I'm certainly glad that it did." Jason took her hand in his and drew it up to place a small kiss on the inside of her wrist.

"What about you?" April asked in a breathless voice, making Jason hard just thinking about all the things he could do to make her sound just like that. "Have you always lived here?"

"No, my brother Donovan and I came from a pack up in Northern Alberta. We've been with our new pack for about five years now."

The waitress brought their meals, and they both dug in with abandon.

"Why did *you* move here?" April asked as she looked at her fork and then finally shook her head and dug into the plate of poutine with her fingers.

Jason looked at the gorgeous woman beside him, licking the gravy off of her fingers and had to struggle to concentrate on what she had just asked him. Obviously, April had no idea what her little display was doing to him.

"Well, my pack…" Jason had been about to answer but stopped himself to look around and see if anyone was sitting close enough to overhear their conversation. "How do you know about wolves anyway?"

"Oh, I was taken in by a really nice family when I was about sixteen." She smiled when she spoke now.

"Long story, but it turned out they were a little different. That's when I found out there was more to the world than most people think there is. They were wolf shifters as well."

Jason's heart broke a little for April at the idea of having to be *taken in* by another family. He wondered where her family was, but decided not to press the issue now. There would be plenty of time to get to know his little mate. He steered the direction of the conversation to the immediate pressing matter instead. "Did she explain how my people find their mates?"

April nodded around a mouthful.

"Well, my brother and I knew that we wouldn't find our mate in the pack we grew up in, and we realized that if we wanted to find her, we needed to get out into the world and track her down. We had met Gabe, our new Alpha, a few weeks after moving to Vancouver, and liked how he ran things down here, so we petitioned to join his pack and he accepted." He then briefly explained his and Donovan's position in the pack.

April's brow furrowed. "You said 'our mate'. You and your brother share a mate then?" she asked, seemingly disappointed with something. "Did you and your brother already find your mate in the pack here?"

"Oh, we found her all right." Jason's smile took on a predatory cast. "But she isn't pack, at least not yet. Not until you meet my brother Donovan and we both claim you as ours."

Chapter Three

"Beta, am I boring you?" Gabe's tone whipped throughout the room, his Alpha essence making it almost impossible to breathe. Donovan looked up from his phone and met the steely gaze of his Alpha and boss. A quick glance at the other senior members of the pack seated around the board table, and he noted that they were all staring at him, most with a look of gleeful anticipation of the verbal smack down and ass kicking Gabe would be serving in his direction momentarily.

"Sorry, Gabe." Donovan held Gabe's gaze as he desperately tried to put his phone back into his jeans pocket without looking or drawing attention to the fact he had the damn thing out in the first place. Normally he wouldn't have replied to his brother's text in a pack meeting, but the message he'd received was the most amazing, most fucking life altering communication in the history of the world.

Jason had found their *mate*. The one woman the fates had destined for them from the moment she was born, just as they had judged them worthy of belonging to her. For a shifter, that was the greatest gift in life and one that should never be taken for granted. When he and Jason had left Alberta five years ago, they had done so to look for their mate. When they met Gabe, they had been instantly drawn to his pack and this area, and now it all made sense why.

A deep rumbling continuous growl rolled through the room and drew Donovan out of his thoughts.

Fuck!

Gabe was not a happy Alpha wolf, and if Donovan didn't get his fucking head on straight, this meeting was going to end with the two of them in wolf form, fighting on the reinforced oak board table. Again.

23

He racked his brain to think about where they had been on the agenda, making an educated guess at what they were talking about. "Patrols on the south side of the city have proved fruitless. There are still humans going missing, but no concrete leads to follow."

There was a chorus of chuckles and jeers from the peanut gallery around him, and Donovan shut them down with a growl of his own.

"You gave that report and we talked about that maybe twenty minutes ago, Beta." Gabe's tone was one that had Donovan's own wolf rising to the surface. "There had better be a damn good reason for you to check out on this meeting and concentrate on your fucking phone, or I will bleed you."

Shit. Donovan did not want to get into it with his Alpha. He had seen the big bastard fight on more than one occasion, and when Donovan was stupid enough to question an order when he was first made Beta, he'd felt the force of Gabe's right hook for himself. Not something he wanted to revisit right in that moment. Especially as he planned to meet his mate as soon as possible. He didn't want to have to face up to April for the first time, black, blue, and smelling like blood.

April. That was the first time he had used her name, and the realization that Jason had found their mate, actually met her face to face and spoke with her to get her name, had Donovan's body filling with shock. *Holy. Shit.* He had a mate, and her name was April.

"Damn, Gabe," Leo, one of the pack's Enforcers, murmured from his place across the table from Donovan. "Donovan just went white as a sheet. Now, we have all faced your wrath in the past, but our wolves usually met it with a thirst to throw down and get bloody. Beta looks like he's just been told he's the father of some random woman's pup."

Leo's brother and Enforcer partner, Ben, who sat sprawled in the chair beside him, barked a laugh and sat forward. "Well, that would certainly explain the lost in thought, goofy expression on his face as well as why he suddenly looks rather ill. Is that it, Donovan? Are you gonna make us all uncles? Leo loves babies. He'd love to babysit for ya." Leo thumped his brother on the chest in the way that all brothers did to convey to their sibling to shut the fuck up.

Not so lost in his epiphany that he couldn't give that the response it deserved, Donovan lifted his right hand and flipped them both off. "Sorry to disappoint you both, but there is no baby. And if there was, I certainly wouldn't trust your hairy asses to look after it."

Another chorus of laughs rocked the room for a brief moment before Gabe let loose the power of his wolf, the room filling with his dominance. Every man around the table became still, the light humor of moments before evaporating beneath the power of the Alpha. Donovan locked gazes with his Alpha as the man stood up slowly from the table.

"Your challenge is accepted, Beta." Gabe's wolf was clear in his voice.

"There was no challenge, Alpha," Donovan spoke as he fought against Gabe's dominance to stand, knowing that if Gabe had not allowed it, he never would have been able to rise. "I will cop to checking out of this meeting for a moment due to a message from my brother that had me distracted, but I most definitely did not challenge you."

Gabe's gaze narrowed, and he slowly removed the shirt he had been unbuttoning as Donovan spoke. "I will concede that no verbal challenge was issued, but you have shown me disrespect in my own fucking office and that is not something I can or will tolerate. I promised Corrine that I wouldn't scratch the shit out of that table anymore. We fight with fists only. Now, get ready. The Enforcers all have to patrol tonight and I know they won't want to miss one second of this one."

The rest of their group clapped and whooped with joy, the bloodthirsty bastards. Donovan sighed in resignation as he removed his own shirt. Gabe was a force to be reckoned with in his wolf form, a fighter of great skill, and one that Donovan had never seen an equal to. The problem was, Gabe fought with his fists even better.

As they all stood, moving the furniture back to make room for his ass kicking, Niall, another Enforcer in the room, asked, "Before Donovan is no longer able to form words, breathe through his nose, and has to eat and drink through a straw for the rest of the week, do we get to find out what the message was?"

Donovan bounced on the balls of his now bare feet, rocking his head from side to side on his shoulders. He glanced at Gabe with a raised eyebrow.

"Go ahead." Gabe waved a hand in his direction. "Answer the question. It makes no difference to me. I've been hungering for a fight for a while now, but with everything going on in the city, I haven't had much time for sparring." Gabe's eyes glittered with anticipation of the fight to come, and that was something Donovan not only knew but respected. They were dominant wolf shifters, and they needed to release some of that energy and aggression that came with the gift of having an animal spirit. And sometimes that meant beating on each other for a while.

Donovan, now just as eager for the fight despite knowing his chances of winning were slim at best, nodded. "Jason has found our mate. Her name is April."

There was a moment of silence just before the room erupted in cheers, and Donovan found himself surrounded by well-wishers. His hand was shaken and his back thumped repeatedly, and he grinned, accepting it all. He knew, just as everyone in the room did, how rare it was.

His pack mates seemed to step back, parting to make room as Gabe stepped forward. Donovan narrowed a look at him slightly as the Alpha's expression was unreadable.

"Congratulations," Gabe said, reaching his hand out in Donovan's direction. "We as a pack look forward to meeting your mate, and I as your Alpha most definitely look forward to welcoming her home." Donovan felt his heart fill with Gabe's words, and he returned the brotherly embrace Gabe gave him. "You and Jason deserve happiness." Gabe pulled back with a grin. "But that still doesn't get you out of the beating you warrant. But it does mean I won't be as hard on you as I might have been."

Donovan laughed. "Fair enough, Alpha. But I should warn you. I'm not sure that I will feel any punches in the euphoric state I'm in."

Gabe's grin broadened, and he dropped into a fighting stance, his body loose, and his hands up to protect his head while his elbows tucked into his sides to guard his ribs. "Well now, a challenge after all! I'll just have to make sure that you do!"

****

An hour later, Donovan slid behind the wheel of his truck with a curse. Gabe had taken it easy on him. That was evident in the fact that Donovan wasn't in the infirmary, but that didn't mean he left him unscathed. His ribs hurt like a motherfucker. When Gabe had declared his punishment over, they had toasted to him and Jason and their good fortune with a fifty-year-old scotch.

His phone vibrated in his pocket just as he tried to gather up the courage to reach over his left shoulder with his right hand for his seatbelt. With a groan, he pushed back against his seat, reaching into his pocket instead to grab his phone. He fumbled to answer the call in his haste to do so when he saw it was Jason.

"Hey," he said into the device.

"Hey back, brother!" Jason's voice rang with happiness on the other end of the line. "Wait until you meet our April. She is so fucking beautiful."

"Where are you? Shall I come there?" Donovan grimaced a little at the needy note in his voice, but screw it, he thought. He wanted to meet the woman destined to be theirs.

"I thought I would bring her by the house. We're at a diner now getting to know each other. I have told her a lot about you. "

"Have you told her about being our mate?" Donovan asked incredulously.

"Yes, and I can understand your hesitation, but," Jason dropped his voice, barely whispering into the phone so that any humans around him wouldn't hear a thing, "she knows about wolves."

"What the hell! How?"

"I know, right? I think she spent most of her life in the system." Donovan's heart ached for the little girl his mate once was, an odd feeling considering he had never met her. "She hasn't told me all the details yet, but she said that a wolf shifter family took her in when she was sixteen and she learned about them that way."

"Well, that makes it easier I guess. You hear a lot of horror stories about women going a little crazy when

they find out their lovers have the ability to shapeshift."
Donovan couldn't even remember the number of men in
his old pack and his current one that had been through a
rough time with their human mates. "What was her
reaction?"

"She excused herself to go to the bathroom. Even
though she knows what we are and how mating among
our kind works, she seemed shocked nonetheless. Oh
shit, here she comes." Jason's voice filled with awe.
"Gods, she is a fucking dream. When she looks at me,
she fills every part of my heart with a light I never knew
existed."

Normally, Donovan would have ribbed and
hassled his brother to no end for spinning such poetic
shit, but hearing him now, and knowing he was looking
at and talking about their mate, filled him with
anticipation and not a small amount of envy.

"Sorry, there was a line for the bathroom," he
heard April say. Donovan closed his eyes at the sound of
her voice over the phone. She sounded like smoke and
sin and had him wanting to sit up and beg.

"That's all right, babe," Jason answered, his voice
slightly quieter as if he was holding the phone away from
him. "I was just talking to my brother. He wants to say hi
to you."

Donovan wanted to do a hell of a lot more than
say hi, but he held his breath waiting. This was the first
time he would speak with his mate, the woman he would
cherish above all others for the rest of his life.

"Hello, Donovan." And that was it. Just the sound
of his name on her lips had Donovan's cock thickening
behind the zipper of his jeans, and his body heating with
the need to get to her.

"Hello, mate."

Chapter Four

Mate. There was that word again. At first, April thought she had misheard Jason when he informed her that she was not only mate to him, but to his brother Donovan as well. Just hearing Donovan's name on Jason's lips stirred feelings in her she could not explain. And Jason … well, she'd had that unexplainable impulse to sniff the gorgeous man earlier, and now, sitting so close to him, she had other urges she had to fight to control, lest they would get her thrown out of the diner.

She couldn't deny their immediate connection, but a huge part of her feared this would turn out be nothing more than a cruel joke. She had seen firsthand what it meant to have a mate, envied it in fact, so the fear that happiness, the kind that she would never have thought possible for herself, would be dangled in front of her here and now, only to be yanked back, terrified her. She immediately had to excuse herself on the pretense of having to use the ladies' room.

"Deep breaths, April, deep breaths," she had chanted in the mirror of the ladies' room. "Great, now I'm talking to myself like a loon."

"Honey, if I came here with a man as fine as that, I'd be all loony, too," came an amused voice from one of the bathroom stalls. She heard a flush and then out stepped the waitress that had served her and Jason. "Hell, if I came here with a beauty like you, I'd also be hyperventilating," she added with a wink.

April felt her cheeks redden, not only from being caught talking to herself but the compliment as well. She wasn't used to it from anyone, even though she knew she wasn't hard on the eyes. The waitress, however, seemed completely unabashed and comfortable in her own skin as she sauntered over to the sink to wash her hands. After drying them, she held out her hand and introduced herself.

"I'm Gina, just in case you were too lost in your hottie's eyes earlier to catch my name when I took your order."

The waitress hit the nail on the head, and it made her cheeks redden even more. Gina also sported a name tag that April hadn't noticed either. April sheepishly took Gina's hand and shook it. "April."

"Well, now I already knew that, seeing as how you talked to yourself and all. What I don't know is why you are in here talking to a mirror instead of that gorgeous specimen out there, who from my experience, and I have a lot of it, looks as if he is completely sweet on you."

April huffed out a breath. She *was* being ridiculous. The man just confessed to being her mate and she ran away like a scared little girl. Well, she was done running away. Something brought her to Vancouver, and now she knew what.

"You're absolutely right," she told Gina.

Jason was on his cell when she reached the table, and the way he smiled at her when they locked gazes had the last of her doubts melting away. They had only just met, and already he looked at her like the sun and moon rose and set with her. She made up a lame excuse about a line in the bathroom, and then he stood up and let her slide back into her seat.

When he handed her the phone to speak with Donovan, her heart did that same beat skipping, heart fluttering action it had done at the club, as if it knew she was about to speak to the other half of her destiny.

"Hello, Donovan," she breathed into the phone, hardly recognizing her own voice.

"Hello, mate." Donovan's voice sounded like smooth velvet in her ear, a mixture of wonder and confidence with a hint of swagger. She couldn't wait to see the face that belonged to his sexy voice.

"I've heard a lot about you, and I … um, well, I … um, can't wait to meet you in person." Both Jason and Donovan chuckled at her clumsily delivered sentence, making her cheeks redden further.

"I can't wait to meet you either, April. You sound lovely."

"Her blush is even lovelier, brother," Jason added. "It complements her beautiful red hair." It didn't surprise April that Jason could hear their conversation even though the phone wasn't up to his ear. She knew that wolves had amazing hearing.

"It just so happens that my favorite color is red," Donovan replied smoothly.

Now April felt the heat on her face for a far different reason other than embarrassment. She watched as Jason's pupils dilated, his nostrils flared, and she heard his low rumbling growl. He knew … he knew exactly what he and his brother were doing to her, and by the slight quirk of his lips, she also knew he seemed pleased.

"What I wouldn't give to be there right now." The longing in Donovan's voice matched her own longing to have them both beside her.

She heard him sigh and then she heard another sound, a fleeting one, but his slight growl from pain was unmistakable to her with her experience. "Are you hurt, Donovan?"

"No, I'm fine, angel," he tried to reassure her, but she wasn't buying it.

Jason held his hand out for the phone. "What happened?" Seconds later, Jason let out a booming laugh.

"All right, all right. I won't." Turning to April, he held the phone out to her and said, "He's fine. Don't worry. He wants to say goodbye to you."

She still wasn't reassured, however. "I don't know if Jason told you," she began when she put the phone back up to her ear, "but I am a nurse. I have experience with shifter physiology as well. I could take a look at you."

"You're a sweetheart, and full of surprises, but really, I will be completely fine." Donovan paused for a moment before adding, "Although, come to think of it, I think I'd like you playing nursemaid."

"Oh … my…" She felt her heart race and the temperature in the room rising with the images his words produced. She couldn't even look at Jason, despite how acutely aware she was of his presence, afraid that she might start removing her clothing right there in the diner.

"I'll see you soon, April."

After they ended the call, April took a few deep breaths to get a hold of herself, and then she passed Jason's phone back to him. She managed to look at him and saw in his eyes what probably reflected in hers—longing and desire.

"Do you have a picture of Donovan?" she croaked out huskily.

Jason searched through his phone and quickly produced a photo of his brother, which only added fuel to her already blazing fire for them both. Donovan was just as gorgeous as his brother.

"I see the resemblance, especially your eyes," she remarked while still admiring his photograph. They had the same cut and color of their eyes, complemented with thick long lashes. Donovan's hair was dark, though, cropped short, in contrast to Jason's lighter, longer locks.

"Smile," Jason said when she finally gave him

back his phone. He took her picture and immediately texted it to Donovan. They both laughed when Donovan texted back three identical emoticons—smiley faces with hearts for eyes. "I think he likes you," Jason added with a wink.

"I like him, too," she replied shyly. "I like you both very much." She must have left her filter at home, she thought. Apparently, she could not contain the thoughts in her head, but fortunately, instead of scaring Jason away, it seemed to be bringing him closer, close enough where she could inch slightly forward and brush her lips against his.

"Will you come home with me, April?" She reveled in the feel of his warm breath against her skin. "Donovan and I will behave. I promise. I just don't think I can bear the thought of saying goodnight to you yet."

"I'm not so sure I could behave, though," she mumbled, but of course, Jason heard her.

He growled low in the back of his throat, and then his lips were on her. Warm soft lips, demanding and hungry for her. She moaned embarrassingly into his mouth when his tongue finally touched hers, but she couldn't care less. She wanted him. Wrapping her arms around his neck, she pulled herself closer to him and deepened their kiss with fervor. Then she felt something completely foreign to her, a tingling in her gums and teeth. Like the impulse she had earlier to inhale his scent, she suddenly wanted to bite. To mark him for the world to see that he belonged to her.

A throat clearing broke the spell and had them both reluctantly pulling apart. "I thought you might like this now," Gina said with a big goofy grin on her face.

She placed the check in front of Jason, who immediately dug into his pocket for his wallet. He threw down some cash, leaving a very generous tip, and grabbed April's hand to help her slide out of the booth.

He continued to hold her hand firmly entwined in his as he led her out of the diner, and they walked in silence toward what she assumed was his car. She couldn't help but steal glances at him along the way, feeling spikes of desire shooting through her entire body. She thought about being wrapped in Jason's arms again and finally coming face to face with Donovan, who she hoped would then wrap her in his arms as well. For the first time in her life, she felt giddy, alive, like she belonged to someone other than herself.

She felt her phone vibrate in her jacket but ignored it as Jason opened up the door to his SUV.

"I think someone really wants you," Jason remarked as they both buckled themselves in and her phone continued to ring.

Dee's number flashed across her screen. "What's up, Dee?" April finally answered. Only it wasn't Dee. It was one of her coworkers calling from Dee's phone frantic and freaking out that Dee had been taken.

"What do you mean taken? Did you call the police?"

"What's going on?" Jason asked. His eyes narrowed suspiciously.

She listened as her coworker, Jessica, April learned her name was, explained. She knew that Jason was listening in as well. Jessica had watched as the man Dee had been dancing with, covered her mouth with some cloth, rendering Dee unconscious. Before Jessica could even react, the man that *she* had been dancing with restrained her. She said that it all happened so fast after that. Both men and Dee along with them had disappeared into the crowd and then out of sight. Dee had left her phone in Jessica's purse since she left her bag at the hospital.

"Why haven't you called the police?" April asked her.

Jessica seemed confused. "I'm not sure … I can't remember why. I can't even remember what they look like anymore."

"Tell her to stay put," Jason commanded. His enforcer side took charge now. "I'm taking you home, April. I need to keep you safe."

"Why? What's happening?"

"I'll explain it all to you later. I promise. I think this has something to do with a case my pack and I are investigating."

"I'm coming with you." No way was she going to let him go back there alone, not when he could be putting himself in danger. And if someone was hurt, she could help.

He turned to face her, his eyes pleading, and he cupped her cheeks. "Please, April. I just found you. I need to keep you safe. Let me take you home."

She looked into Jason's face, trying to discern his intent, and after a moment nodded. It seemed she would not be able to refuse him anything. She directed him to her house located less than a ten-minute drive from the diner. He walked her up to her apartment, waited until she unlocked the door, and kissed her quickly but thoroughly.

"Promise me you won't go back out tonight. Promise me, April."

"Okay, I promise."

He kissed her forehead before leaving her.

****

The next morning, after a completely sleepless night, she found herself sick with worry at the hospital.

She couldn't concentrate on anything and kept excusing herself, claiming that she wasn't feeling well. Everyone assumed it was because of Dee. Word had spread that she had gone missing. April worried about Dee, but it was nothing compared to her fear that something must have happened to Jason. She kept berating herself all night that she hadn't taken his or Donovan's number before Jason had left.

"I'm so stupid," she continued to chide herself. Everything just happened so fast. She didn't think it through. With no idea where they lived and no wolf contacts in Vancouver to help her locate their Alpha, Gabe, she was at a loss for what to do.

By the time her shift had ended, she felt ready to crawl out of her skin. She'd only promised Jason to stay put last night. She made no such promises tonight. She quickly changed out of her scrubs, knowing that her plain looking clothes would make her stick out like a sore thumb at Wave, but she couldn't bring herself to care. The club would be her starting point.

The place was fairly empty when she arrived, being that it was still early. She made a beeline for the bar, recognizing the bartender from the night before. Again, she berated herself for not thinking ahead. She wished that she had taken a photo of Jason on her phone right after he took one of her on his. Now she had no photo to show the bartender, only his description to give.

"Why are you looking for him?" the bartender asked suspiciously.

April felt the hairs on the back of her neck stand up as if in warning. She knew she felt something off about the bartender yesterday, but couldn't put her finger on it.

"Oh, I just thought he was cute," she lied. "Was hoping I'd run into him again."

"Didn't I see you leave with him last night?"

Shit. "Um … never mind."

She tried to back up slowly but found herself colliding with a hard muscular chest. When she turned around a tall, beefy man was sneering at her, like she was something distasteful to him. She felt the hairs on her neck stand again in warning. His almost black eyes peered at her, searching, for what, she did not know.

April found herself standing frozen, a feeling she wasn't entirely sure was hers. She wanted to run, she wanted to scream, hell, she wanted to reach out, kick the guy in the balls and get the hell out of there, but something in his eyes held her still. She cringed when he reached for her face and slowly drew a finger down her cheek. She felt a small shock of electricity as his skin made contact with her own.

"Ah, the one that slipped away last night." His sneer morphed into a cruel smile and told her that whatever he searched for, he had found.

April found herself being hauled out of the bar by him and two other men. She tried to scream, but some sort of block in her vocal chords prevented her from doing so. No one at the club even seemed to notice that she was being dragged away against her will. And there was that damn blue light again, sparking from her palms. She needed to finally admit to herself that she wasn't just imagining it. It was real, and she needed to figure out what *it* was.

They led her to the back entrance, her struggles amounting to nothing, and onto a side street where a black limo awaited. The beefy goon smiled once more at her, and then he shoved her inside the car where she came face to face with an unconscious Jason.

Chapter Five

"Oh my God, what have you bastards done to him?"

Jason could hear April's panicked voice as his mind slowly tried to shake the groggy haze from whatever those Fae assholes had used to knock him out. He'd gone back to the bar after dropping April safely off at home, and apparently he'd asked the wrong bartender too many questions. He followed the guy to a back office, and the next thing he knew, he was waking up in some cheap limo, his wolf frantic, telling him not only had he been sleeping for almost an entire day, but that now their mate had been captured as well. Trussed up and barely conscious, neither he nor his wolf could protect her.

"Oh, do calm yourself, girl," he heard a male voice say. It sounded like the guy sat across from him. Jason didn't recognize the voice of the male speaking, and his accent was clearly not from around here. "Your dog isn't dead. There's no need for hysterics." The man paused for a moment as if contemplating something. "You almost had us fooled, you know, clever girl. None of our trackers could scent you with the stench of your beast overwhelming us, but you can't hide the spark of Fae blood in your eyes, not from Frederych at least."

"What are you talking about?" April asked as she searched Jason's now blinking eyes for any signs of trauma. "I am not Fae. What could you possibly want with me?"

"April?" Jason finally struggled to sit up and take in the scene before him. "Are you all right? Did they hurt you, baby?"

"No, I'm okay," she answered huddling in closer to him. "Are you okay? I couldn't find any bumps on your head. How do you feel?"

They both looked over at the tall man sitting across from them when he sighed dramatically.

"So touching, really. The love between mates," the stranger said right before he rolled his eyes.

"Who the *fuck* are you, and what do you want with us?" Jason growled, his wolf so close to the surface he was barely understandable.

"I am Kheelan, the captain of the Fae King's royal guard, so watch your tone, *boy*," the man sneered. "And it's not you we want, *dog*. Your little pretty there has led us on quite a merry chase from her last hometown."

Jason had never been this close to any Fae before. It shocked him that they would make such a bold move against the pack as to kidnap two of its members. Something big must really be brewing for them to risk Gabe's wrath. He took a closer look at the Fae in front of him. Kheelan was very tall but had a more streamlined build than shifters did, and there was no denying the Fae were a beautiful race. Too bad most of the ones he'd met so far turned out to be such absolute dicks.

"Why were you tracking her?"

Kheelan looked back at Jason for a moment with a scowl, before a smarmy grin replaced it, and he answered, "My King has but to ask, and I will provide."

That still didn't answer his question, and the avoidance made his wolf nervous. What could the False Fae King possibly want with April, and what made him think she was Fae? He certainly couldn't smell it on her. Jason looked over at his mate. He could see the fear in her eyes, and it almost killed him. He'd only known her for two days, and already he was failing her. He did not deserve a mate as perfect as she was.

"Why me?" April asked in a whisper.

"Well, my dear, you weren't very selective in who you *helped* along the way." He smirked at her, and Jason had no idea what this bastard was implying when he said "helped" like it was a dirty thing. "You have no idea how many humans we had to endure to get to the right one." Kheelan scrunched his nose in distaste. "But you animals do so love to gossip. The peculiar thing, though, was that *you* were the only one who didn't seem to know you were doing anything at all. Didn't you ever wonder why they all came to you for their bumps and bruises, my dear? Did you think it was your charming nursing skills?" Kheelan threw in an amused laugh, like one would when a child had done or said something silly. "From there, all it took was a short trip and a little torture to find out where the little nurse had moved her traveling sideshow to … and how thoughtful of you to consider our convenience by moving closer to home for us. So thank you, my dear, for saving us the trouble."

What the hell? All this time they had been taking humans to find April? Jason turned over Kheelan's words, letting them sink into his still groggy brain. *Our mate is not only possibly Fae but also a … healer?* Something else Kheelan had said registered in his brain as well—"the stench of your beast overwhelming us". It made sense that his wolf and that of her wolf family could have hidden her scent all of these years, but something still didn't add up.

April must have read the shocked look on his face because she grabbed his arm immediately and blurted out, "I don't know what he's talking about, Jason. I can't be one of them. He's crazy. The wolves just came to me because I was the only nurse they knew within the pack. That's all."

"April, you're our mate," Jason said quietly

trying to ignore the impatient, disgusted sounds coming from the bastard Fae across from them. "We accept you as you are. That's all we'll ever need. I don't care if you turn out to be a troll."

"There are trolls, too?" she asked, her eyes widening.

"Good Goddess, I can't take this anymore." Kheelan banged on the partition, and the window quickly lowered, revealing two more Fae in the front of the car. "How much longer until we reach the forest? These two are making me gag, and we used up the last of the sleeping draught keeping the wolf down overnight."

"Ten more minutes, Captain," the driver answered.

"Good, now, you two shut up or I start peeling skin," Kheelan ordered before he closed his eyes and let his head rest back against the seat.

****

Ten minutes later, the car came to a stop. As soon as the back door opened, Jason could smell the forest. His wolf fought even harder against the ropes binding his hands and feet. He was glad that the Fae hadn't bound April, but he knew why, of course. They were confident that she wouldn't try to escape, leaving her mate to their mercy, although he wished that she would.

"We're going to untie your legs, dog, but if you try anything, your woman will bear the punishment." Kheelan motioned for the guard to untie his feet as he grabbed April's arm and hauled her outside. "Are we clear?"

Jason simply nodded, his wolf too close to the surface in his rage. His incisors had dropped, and he didn't want to give the bastard any excuse to hurt his mate.

"Get walking, you two. I want to cross the Veil in time for dinner." Kheelan pushed Jason towards a well-worn path through the trees. "The food you barbarians eat on this side is disgusting. No wonder human lives are so short and they age so quickly."

"Where are you taking us?" April whimpered as she clung to Jason's arm, trying to keep up with the guard in front of them in the fading light of the forest.

"Why, I'm taking you home, child. I didn't tell you that I knew your parents before they died, did I?" Kheelan answered in a frightening tone, putting his finger to his chin as if he were trying to recall having that particular conversation. "Oh yes, I knew your father *very* well indeed, my dear. Reysken and I began our guard training at the same time, and we were the best of friends. He was mine in *all* ways."

"What?" April stopped walking and just stared at the cruel man in front of her. "You knew my parents? You're lying!"

"Of course, that was before your *whore* mother, Ilyra, came along with her tainted bloodline and her filthy magic." Kheelan just carried on with his super-villain diatribe, like he was giving an interview as only a true sociopath could. "Reysken would have trusted *me* with his secrets if not for her."

April gasped at the way this monster spoke about her parents. Jason's heart broke for her as he saw the grief and rage sweep across her features. He wondered if Kheelan spoke the truth or if he simply said those things to taunt her.

"Imagine my surprise finding you. I recognize your father's scent on you," Kheelan laughed as they arrived at a large clearing that butted up against a large bare stone mountainside. "The Goddess is rewarding me for my dedication."

"You asshole!" April screamed as she launched herself at Kheelan before Jason could get in front of her. "Shut your filthy lying mouth!"

"You're pathetic." The Fae caught and slapped her before she could do any damage to him. He then pushed her down as the other two Fae tried their damnedest to hang onto Jason as he fruitlessly tried to get to April.

Kheelan quickly went up to the rock surface and began to trace symbols into the air. Then, all of a sudden, the hair on the back of Jason's neck stood up and his wolf began to whimper in his head that something was very wrong.

"Throw him through the portal. I'm hungry," he heard Kheelan say behind him before he was shoved towards the rock wall and everything went dark.

Chapter Six

"Damn, baby, you are just how I like 'em," the heavily made up and perfumed blonde in front of him slurred drunkenly. "Tall, built like a linebacker, and ready to be fucked hard. You want me to fuck you hard, lover?" The woman then had the audacity to run her long, red tipped nails down Donovan's chest.

He snatched her hand from him, flinging it away in distaste. Donovan growled low, his eyes no doubt changing to reflect the fact that his wolf hovered just beneath the surface, both of them furious that some woman would dare put her hands on him. He had a mate, and the touch of any other woman would not be tolerated.

The blonde's eyes widened in terror. "Hey, I'm sorry. I ... um, didn't mean anything by it." The woman sounded surprisingly more sober than she had just moments before, and then she scurried away.

Donovan was moments away from shifting, screaming, or beating the shit out of the next person to touch him, look at him wrong, or shit, even breathe in his direction. He was pissed. He was frustrated that every place he looked, every lead he followed turned up nothing. Jason was missing, and he didn't mind admitting to the fact that it worried him. Add to that, he had no way of contacting April. Human girls had been going missing in increasing numbers, and he feared for her safety.

After the call the night before last to introduce him to their mate, Donovan had been secretly planning their first face to face meeting. He wanted to make the best impression he could on their new mate. Jason had told him that she was beautiful, but after seeing the photo he had texted him, the word beautiful seemed inadequate. He made a mental note to one day memorize every single freckle that adorned her nose and lovely blushing cheeks. As soon as he had heard her voice on the phone, his dick had jumped to fully aroused in seconds.

He'd rushed home filled with hope that Jason would be able to convince April to come home with him. Donovan wanted to clean up a little after the beating he'd taken from Gabe. He'd jumped in the shower, which led to him missing the next call from Jason. Apparently a friend of April's had been taken, and Jason was heading back to the area the bar was in to see if he could find anything.

Donovan had called him back immediately afterward, but Jason hadn't picked up. He also hadn't told Donovan in his message what bar he was going to look in either, so Donovan spent the rest of that night going from bar to bar searching.

He'd given up in the early hours of the morning, and headed home, truly expecting to find Jason passed out on his bed, having lost his phone somewhere. When he found nothing, he convinced himself that Jason was still searching, or the lucky bastard had returned to the arms of their mate. A move he envied, but couldn't blame his brother for if that was in fact what he had done. Jason was an Enforcer for the largest wolf pack in North America and there was no way there could be a nefarious explanation, he convinced himself.

In the afternoon, Donovan had gone searching again, this time promising himself that once he found his little brother, he'd show him with both fists why Donovan was Beta. The little prick was being a douchebag by not checking in. He'd been searching for hours and still turned up nothing. He went back home, hoping once again that Jason would somehow be there waiting, but again, he only found an empty house and

Jason's phone had been going straight to voicemail. He was just about to report the fact that Jason was missing, when Gabe called, letting him know there was an even more unusual amount of Fae activity happening downtown and it correlated with more missing humans.

Seven hours later, Donovan fell into bed exhausted. He and Niall had only managed to clear four bars in that time. Between them, they had tangled with no fewer than seven Fae who each decided it was better to mess with them then to leave quietly. Bastards. A couple of them got in a few cheap shots, and Donovan sported cuts and bruises he hadn't before when he crawled out of bed that afternoon.

When he awoke and still found no sign of Jason, he barely kept his shit together. He had made the decision to go to Gabe with this despite the whole Fae uprising bullshit when his phone rang.

"Jason?" He answered quickly, without even glancing at the screen.

"No, it's Niall." The soft Irish brogue in his friend's voice told Donovan Niall was stressed about something.

"What's happening?"

"I'm at the edge of the forest just south of Gabe's, and one of those Fae bastards is here." Niall spoke quietly into the phone.

Donovan frowned as he grabbed his keys and made for his truck. "Just standing there? What the fuck do you think he wants?"

"Pizza," Niall shot back sarcastically. "I don't fucking know, Donovan, and because in your infinite wisdom you decreed that we had to approach these fuckers in pairs, I'm calling you, because my brothers are still in Toronto!"

Donovan growled low down the phone, his wolf

unhappy at the tone Niall had taken. "Was that a challenge? Because the way things have been going these last few days, I will kill that Fae then use you to wipe up the blood."

Niall sighed. "No, shit! Sorry, Beta, it was not a challenge. My wolf is pissed this fucker is standing anywhere near our Alpha's home. I can't get a hold of Gabe, and everything in me wants to rip this fucker to pieces."

Donovan pressed his foot harder on the accelerator, the V8 engine jumping to do his bidding. "I'll be there in two minutes."

As it turned out, the Fae had been sent here with a message for Gabe and wasn't at all keen to share it with him instead. Donovan had taken him to Gabe's and let the fucker give his message. Alefric, the King of the Fae was giving them forty-eight hours to return a Fae woman to his realm or war was to be waged. The woman he wanted returned was none other than the newly found mate of two of his fellow pack-mates, Leo and Ben Eklund. Suffice it to say, the messenger got the answer that kind of request deserved.

Gabe ripped his arm off, and Donovan and Niall chewed on him a bit before leaving him in the forest where his scent trail had led them. Actually, they chewed on him a lot, and he was definitely in more pieces now than he'd been when he'd first delivered his message, but if the Fae found him sooner rather than later, there'd still be something left of him to find instead of ash.

Despite the fact he'd been able to release some of his pent-up rage on the messenger, he was still frustrated as hell that he couldn't find Jason and had no way of locating April. He headed back out in search of his brother. The classless blonde would have offended him on a good day, so unlucky for her, she had crossed paths with him tonight. And he was getting sick of listening to music that was playing too loud, drinks that were watered down, and women who thought they had a right to touch him.

"I'll take a beer," he all but growled at the bartender. He looked about as interested in serving him a beer as Donovan was in drinking it, but he had to keep up appearances.

As he lifted the bottle to his lips to take a drink, his phone vibrated in his pocket. He growled in frustration and relief when he read his brother's name on the display. Donovan pushed his way into the corridor that led to the bathrooms and took the exit that opened into the alleyway behind the bar before he answered the call.

"Jason, you arrogant little fuck, where the hell are you?" Donovan asked in the way of greeting. "You better have a damned good reason for going stealth for the last forty-eight hours, you prick, otherwise, I won't just put you on your ass, I'll make fucking sure you stay there for a good while."

There was silence at the end of the phone that had the hair on the back of Donovan's neck standing on end.

"My, my, is that how all dogs speak to each other or is that simply a brother thing?" The voice was clearly not his brother on the other end of the phone.

"Who is this?" Donovan's voice was little more than a growl.

Jason had taken a photo of their mate last night on his phone. That image would be proof of the woman that could bring them both to their knees. He wouldn't part with the device easily. If this bastard had it then Jason hadn't given it to him willingly.

"Let's just say that I am someone you are about to

become *very* open and honest with," the smarmy voice replied with a hint of triumph to it that had Donovan's wolf pacing within him.

"Well, in the spirit of being open and honest, I think it is only fair to warn you. There are only a few people in this world that I give a shit about. The owner of the phone you've decided to give me this little courtesy call on happens to be one of them, and if you've hurt him in any way, then you and I are going to have a very different future relationship, one that ends with you meeting me, and me introducing you to the body bag you'll be requiring for the duration of your stay above ground."

At the sound of the bastard's laugh down the phone, Donovan's phone creaked in his hand as his grip tightened. "I do so love how you shifters immediately turn to threatening death or dismemberment when confronted with a superior being who holds all the cards."

He knows about shifters? Superior being? "Not only are you a huge narcissistic asshole, but you are a *deluded* narcissistic asshole. I reckon when I meet you and take you out of this world kicking and screaming, effectively removing you from any future gene pool, I'll be doing all of human and shifter kind one hell of a favor."

"As if I would ever deign to breed with one of your kind," the guy snapped, for the first time displaying something more than that smug condescension he'd been using. "And human? Goddess, no! I am Fae, dog, and I would not want to dilute our kind with the likes of you and yours."

He knew immediately that it could not be a coincidence that this guy was Fae. Donovan didn't believe in coincidences. "So tell me, asshole, why in the fuck would you think you hold all the cards?"

"Because, *you worthless mutt*," he spat the last word, "I have your dog brother and the bitch your kind call mate."

Donovan's heart stilled in his chest for a brief moment before it came pounding back to life. "You listen to me you, nameless fuck, I—"

"No, dog, you will listen to me!" the man interrupted, his voice rising.

Despite every cell in Donovan's body demanding that he roar, rage, and threaten the man who had his brother and his mate, he bit his tongue and listened.

"Last night, two of your kind found a woman they believe to be their mate, and will no doubt want to *claim* her. We do not want that to happen. We want her back in our realm as quickly as possible. You, Beta to the Alpha known as Gabe, will make sure to deliver her, or I will make you regret it."

Different prick, same threat. Donovan was really getting sick of this Alefric guy and his drones.

Donovan's growl of rage was insistent, and he had to swallow it back in order to speak. "If you hurt her…"

"What will you do?" The smug as shit tone was back. "I told you before that I hold all the cards. You asked me my name before, dog, and I will give it to you now, not because you demanded it, but because I want you to know the name of the Fae that will end your brother and your mate if you do not do as I have commanded. I am the Captain of the Fae King's guard. My name is Kheelan Falk, and if you do not answer this phone when I call it, your brother and your mate will be harmed. If you fail to do what my King has decreed and what I have requested, then your mate will die with my name on her lips as she screams and begs me for mercy to end her quickly. Test me if you will, Beta, but be it on your head."

The click of the phone as he disconnected sounded like a gunshot and Donovan roared his mate's name to the heavens, fighting the urge to crush the phone to oblivion. He was a hair's breadth from shifting. For a less dominant wolf, the urge to do so would have been impossible to stop, but there was a reason Donovan was Beta. He was stronger than any other wolf in the pack apart from Gabe.

Donovan spun in the alley, striding out to the curb where he'd parked his truck. He had to think. He headed back to Gabe's, hoping he could formulate a plan that would enable him to save his mate and his brother, and get Donovan within striking distance of this Fae.

There was another reason why Donovan had risen to Beta in his pack. He proved to be one of the deadliest fighters, a trait he was very much looking forward to impressing upon the walking dead man, this Fae called Kheelan.

Chapter Seven

April sat huddled in a corner of her darkened cell, her head resting on her knees. Jason was quiet now, probably passed out from the pain, she figured. He tried to talk to her sometimes through the other side of the wall in between the beatings, and it broke her heart not only from how much pain had been inflicted upon him but the fact that he tried to talk through it to her, hoping to convince her it didn't hurt that much.

"Please, Jason," she had cried. "Save your strength."

They hadn't even let her see him since they got to this wretched place. The vile Kheelan and his goons had marched them straight to the palace after she had launched herself at him, trying to hurt him. She saw that same blue spark emit from her palms again, but Kheelan seemed unfazed.

They shoved Jason in a cell first and then pushed her forward down the tunnels, turning several times until they reached another door. Just minutes after they had secured her inside, she'd been frantically looking for a way out when the first sounds of Jason's abuse came through a small grated air vent in the back far corner of the cell. For hours and hours, she cried as that bastard Kheelan took delight in doing whatever it took to wring pained screams out of her mate. April had never felt so helpless in all of her life, and she was terrified that they would kill him. On the walk over to her prison, she had overheard one guard telling the other that Jason's bonds would prevent him from shifting fully, which also would stop him from healing as well.

How she wished that she could free him from his bonds. She had seen what wolves were capable of when they were in a full shifted form. Jason could have probably obliterated the lot of them before more guards could arrive to stop him. Now, even if somehow she managed to escape and free Jason, there were way too many Fae to take on even in his wolf form. She had gone over scenario after scenario of escape plans, even a few carefully whispered ones with Jason once he'd assured her that Fae do not have the kind of hearing that wolves do, only to come up empty every time.

So instead of escaping, she cried and screamed and clawed at the wall when they came to beat him. "Stop it! I'll fucking kill you all," she had promised. The fact that she meant it had surprised the hell out of her. She'd hated people before. Her cruel foster parents, several of them in fact, and the hunters who liked to shoot wolves back in her former town, just to name a few, but never had she thought herself capable of actually taking another life. She thirsted for blood now. Something inside of her was practically demanding it.

She also thought about Donovan in those moments. April knew that he must be going out of his mind. Without ever even meeting him, just from how Jason spoke of him, she knew Donovan would never stop searching for them. She only hoped that it wouldn't be their corpses that he would find.

A noise from down the hall snapped her out of her reverie. Then she saw the cell door directly in front of her open. Two guards she did not recognize unceremoniously shoved a woman with short dark hair inside and then they left without saying a word. The stranger looked completely unafraid, like being in the cell of some sort of medieval looking dungeon was no big deal for her. Although she did scrunch up her nose in distaste. April couldn't blame her. The stench in here was godawful.

She then watched the attractive woman pace her cell continuously until something she had said caught April's interest.

"Donovan had better get my message to my mates."

"Donovan? Do you mean Donovan Olson?" April asked her, still keeping herself hidden.

"I'm not sure what his last name is, but if I said the word Beta, what would that mean to you?"

April gasped. This woman knew Donovan. She immediately got up and moved to the front of her cell. "That is my Donovan's rank. His Alpha is a wolf by the name of Gabe Errikson."

"That's him," the woman replied with a smile. "He's your mate?"

"Yes, he is, one of them, and we haven't, um, well—*you know*." April felt her cheeks redden from her confession. She wondered if there was no end to her verbal diarrhea from the last few days.

"You haven't claimed each other," the dark haired woman acknowledged with an amused smile, "but that's okay. I knew my men were meant for me before we, *you knowed*, too. What is your name, and how in the hell did you end up down here?"

"My name is April, and Jason and I were taken from the earth realm and brought here. They have been torturing J-Jason." April's voice caught on her mate's name, and it felt as if her heart was bleeding. "But they aren't even asking him any questions. Who the hell does that? Interrogates a man without actually asking any questions?"

"Is he in there with you?" the woman asked, peering into her cell.

"No, they have him on the other side of the wall," April replied, her voice trembling. "I hear him shouting and growling, but they won't let me see him." She left out the part about being able to talk to him just in case the woman in front of her was some kind of spy. With the ordeal she and Jason found themselves in, her brain was telling her to be suspicious of everyone, even though April's instincts were urging her to trust the stranger.

She immediately felt bad about her paranoia when the woman held her hand out. April reached out until they were able to clasp hands. When they finally touched, a blue light sparked between their palms. They both gasped and pulled back their hands, staring at each other with wide eyes.

"You are a healer?" the woman whispered in shock.

April frowned in confusion and then anger. She wondered if there would ever come a day when she knew more about herself than apparently other people did. She decided to trust the kind woman. Maybe she'd even be able to help April figure out the truth about herself. "I don't kn—"

The sound of the door at the end of the hall slamming open interrupted them.

"Get back," the woman ordered quietly.

April immediately faded into the darkest corner of her cell and observed the woman as she took on a disinterested appearance. Kheelan strode up to the woman's cell without even sparing April a second glance and announced that the king would speak with her. They had an argument about using shackles. The woman easily won, impressing the hell out of April and even giving her a bit of added courage. And by their exchange, April also got the impression that she wasn't the only one who would be doling out some justice to Kheelan when she got the chance.

The woman nearly stumbled out of her cell, but immediately straightened up and winked in April's direction. April then watched as the woman strode out of there with her held head high, like she owned the place. Damn, she was going to have to get her number when all of this was over, she thought. She may have just found her new best friend.

She was just about to see if Jason had woken up when his loud cries informed her that he in fact, was awake and they were hurting him again. She ran to the wall and banged on it repeatedly, not caring about her bloody fists.

"Damn you!" she screamed. "Just leave him alone."

She slid down the wall, gasping for air and feeling so completely helpless. "Just leave him alone," she whispered.

She gently placed her hand against the wall, this time pretending it was Jason she was touching and comforting instead of some cold stone. "I'm so sorry," she sobbed. "I'm so, so sorry. It's my fault. It's all my fault." She banged against the wall again and shouted, "It's me you wanted. Well, I am fucking right here!"

Her sobs were uncontrollable now, choking her with every blow she heard them deliver to Jason.

"It's not your fault, angel," came a familiar whispered voice, startling her.

She swiped at her blurry eyes and immediately recognized the speaker crouching low in front of her cell. "Donovan?" she breathed. She had thought she heard a growl earlier when the woman stumbled out of her cell but figured she had only imagined it. That it had only been wishful thinking.

She crawled over to him, not trusting her legs to be strong enough to stand. She got as close to the metal bars as she could, and Donovan slid his hands through them, hugging her to him as much as the bars between them allowed.

"They won't stop hurting him," she whispered.

A particularly loud scream from Jason had them both flinching, and April watched as tears slid down Donovan's cheeks. He then tried to pick the locking mechanism on the door.

"Do you know which of these tunnels lead to the other side of the wall?" he asked her in a rushed frustrated whisper when the lock wouldn't budge.

April nodded and pointed in the direction of one of the furthermost tunnels. She also explained that she had observed the direction Kheelan had come from after the first time he hurt Jason. He had come to taunt her with the blood of her mate on his hands. Donovan let out a low furious growl in response.

"And you?" he asked, his wolf rising to the surface. "Have they hurt you?"

"Not physically, no."

"Sit tight, my angel. I am going to go rip apart the men hurting my brother, get their keys, and then Jason and I will come and get you." He then cupped her cheek, bringing her face closer to him, and kissed her lips tenderly.

"Donovan," she began after he released her reluctantly and stood up, "make it hurt."

With a slight quirk to his lips, he nodded and ran off in Jason's direction, disappearing from sight.

Then all hell broke loose as the ground beneath her began to violently shake.

Chapter Eight

Jason drifted in and out of consciousness as he hung from the shackles on the cold, damp wall. He'd tried to keep track of how long he and April had been captured, but after the first day of torture, it had become a blur. That Fae bastard certainly hadn't been kidding when he'd threatened to peel them in the car. He was a sadistic fuck, and Jason was only praying that they would concentrate on him and leave April unharmed.

When Kheelan had first arrived and watched as the guards secured him to the wall, he'd slowly undone his jacket and shirt, placing them on a bench in the corner. For a moment, Jason had grown concerned what his intentions might be, but those fears were quickly abated by Kheelan's mocking laughter.

"Like I would lower myself by lusting after a beast," Kheelan sneered as he walked over to a cabinet and perused its contents. "I have a King's bed to go to when I'm done here, dog. *You,* I just need for the sweet sounds of your pain."

Jason had held up pretty well when the two guards had just beat him for the first couple of hours before they shackled him to the wall. He was after all a wolf. He had also been able to hear the soft crying of his mate from an open grate on the other side of the wall, and the last thing he wanted to do was worry her. Unfortunately, when Kheelan had stepped in, things had escalated quickly, and no matter how hard he tried to keep from screaming out as the fucker meticulously broke each of his fingers slowly, seeming to savor the expressions of pain that crossed his face with the snap of each bone, he ended up losing control.

"How curious," Kheelan had remarked nonchalantly as he snapped the last finger on Jason's left hand. He seemed fascinated by the half-shift changes in Jason's body in reaction to the pain. "Does it cause you even more discomfort to not be able to shift fully according to your instincts?"

A low growl escaped Jason's throat, and his electric blue wolf eyes narrowed at the male in front of him.

"I was initially skeptical at what the magic users told me, about how their binding cuffs would affect shifters, but they do seem to be keeping your beast at bay, don't they?" Kheelan mused as he picked up a small, thin knife and approached Jason once more. "Why don't we see just how strong they are now?"

Jason didn't feel the knife enter the skin on his chest, that's how sharp it was, but he did smell the coppery tang of his own blood, as well as the pressure against his flesh and then the piercing burn of his nerve endings followed as Kheelan slipped the blade under the skin and sliced through it. He had never known that kind of pain existed as he did the second the Fae grabbed the flap of skin and slowly began to draw it back, using his knife to ensure a straight line as though he were skinning a salmon.

Jason's screams filled the air as his torture continued until he finally passed out. The sound of April yelling out his name was the last thing he clung to before the darkness claimed him.

****

Taunting, followed by several sharp, successive jabs to his open wounds, abruptly brought Jason awake. He heard April's screams again, a sound that gutted him even more than the pain being inflicted upon him. Then he heard another sound—the rumbling of the stone walls around him. He was still groggy from blood loss, so he thought he was imagining it at first, but then, the floor also began shaking, the ceiling began raining dust and chunks of rock and rubble down, causing the two guards to finally cease beating him.

"What the hell is going on up there?" the Fae guard, who moments ago had been beating on him, asked his partner standing at the cell door. "The alarm has been tripped. We should be up there protecting the King, not down here with a half-dead dog," he finished with disgust.

"We stay where the Captain told us to," the other one answered as they braced themselves for another shake of the palace walls.

It sounded like the castle was going to crumble down around them, and Jason almost wished it would if only for the reason that Kheelan wouldn't be able to inflict any more damage on him. He winced as pain assaulted him, and when he looked down at his chest and stomach, he saw a mass of blood and open flesh. It almost seemed as though the sadistic son of a bitch was trying to create some sort of pattern by removing large strips of Jason's skin.

Shit. No wonder he had passed out. Even a wolf couldn't maintain consciousness after losing this amount of blood. It was everywhere, covering his entire lower body and pooling out around him on the cold stone floor.

Oh Goddess, April!

Kheelan had gone, and Jason could only hope that he still left her alone. Fortunately, the only screams he had heard coming from April's cell were the ones she uttered on his behalf. He tried to bring his wolf to the surface, straining to see if he could hear her through the grate, but the shaking and rumbling of the palace was making it impossible to hear anything but the grumbling of his two guards.

Then Jason did hear the most wonderful sound, a low growl from his brother's wolf. He'd heard that same sound a million times as they hunted together, usually right before his big brother ripped into their prey.

"There's something out there. I can hear it," the Fae guard said, peering into the hall as he opened up the cell door.

"Then go and deal with it, you idiot," the one closer to him responded as he looked up in fear toward the protesting ceiling. "Kheelan will have *us* chained to the wall if we leave his prisoner."

Jason's wolf had finally decided to join the party, pacing in his head, telling him that this quake and the shaking of the palace weren't natural, that there was magic being used here.

"You should have left with your friend," Jason said quietly, trying to pull himself up to stand against the wall.

"I do not fear an earthquake, *dog*. This palace has stood for thousands of years." The guard sneered at him before he turned back to face the now open cell door. "You should be more worried about yourself with the amount of blood Kheelan has taken from you."

"He didn't mean you should fear the earthquake, fucker," came Donovan's voice, just before he finally appeared in the doorway, his low growl rumbling over the sound of crumbling stone. "You're going to lose more than blood now that I see what you've done to my brother."

The guard's eyes went wide at seeing Donovan covered in blood. Jason was fairly certain that the Fae scum figured out that the blood belonged to his partner. Donovan stepped fully into the cell and then shifted into a huge black wolf. He leaped at the Fae guard, whose arms came up to cover his face, a fatal mistake as the move left his chest and stomach open to attack. Donovan took full advantage. Jason watched without pity or remorse as his brother ripped and tore at the male until he was a bleeding pile of flesh on the stone floor.

"Donovan," he finally said once the man was most certainly dead, "we need to get out of here and get April."

The black wolf finally looked up from the gore, and then Donovan shifted back, rushing to Jason's side with a tormented look on his face as he took in the damage that had been done.

"Goddess, Jason," Donovan whispered in horror. "What did he do to you?"

"Just get something to undo these cuffs. I need to shift a few times so I can stop some of this bleeding and begin to heal, but these are some kind of magically enhanced metal that prevented me from shifting."

Donovan looked through the dead guard's bloody clothes until he finally found a key ring that unlocked the bindings. As soon as Jason's wrists were free, his wolf exploded from his skin and he collapsed to the floor in exhaustion. And then a piercing scream from April assaulted his ears. She was calling out to them for help.

"Fuck," Donovan muttered as he knelt beside him. "Shift back, brother. Hurry and I'll help you walk. April is in danger."

When Jason shifted back to his human skin, at least the blood had stopped gushing from the wounds on his front. Kheelan was a sadistic fuck, however because he must have been using some sort of poisoned or cursed blade as the actual open cuts had not gotten any smaller.

"Let's go get our mate. I can't hear her over all this racket." Jason leaned against his brother as they left the cell. "What the hell do you think is going on up there?"

"War, brother," Donovan replied, "we've brought war to these bastards."

Chapter Nine

"Calm yourself, brother," Donovan murmured, speaking low so that only Jason could hear him. "We're only staying until the formalities are over, and then we will resume the hunt."

Jason stood beside him, holding himself so tense that his entire body seemed to tremble, and Donovan could hear a low continuous growl rumbling through his brother's chest. Despite Jason's denials, Donovan knew the damage that had been done to him in the dungeons the day Erica reclaimed her rightful place in this realm two weeks ago, left him in constant pain. Erica had attempted to heal the wounds on his chest several times, but they hadn't healed as they should have. The shifting powers of Jason's wolf and the ancient healing powers of the Fae weren't enough to help him either. Donovan heard Jason take two deep breaths, and his trembling ceased for the moment.

The two of them stood in the rear of the crowd that had gathered in the throne room of the palace to witness the coronation of the new queen. Erica sat on the throne at the front, Ben and Leo beside her, while a gray haired old dude stood chanting and moving his arms around in what Donovan suspected was an ancient ritual appropriate for such a formal event. To Donovan, though, he looked like he was swatting at some annoying insect.

When Erica looked out over the crowd and caught his eye, her expression turned sad, but then she lifted her chin with an inner strength he had come to respect in the diminutive woman. She had lived through the pain and danger that had followed her since she watched her parents murdered in cold blood right in front of her as a child, and she had even graciously forgiven Donovan for his role in returning her to face Alefric, a true testament to who she was and how she would lead her people. Donovan dipped his head in acknowledgment almost at the same time as Jason. Erica sent them both a small smile, but the sorrow never left her face completely.

Erica had met April that same day that he'd first come face to face with his mate in the dungeons, and during their conversation, Erica discovered that not only was their beautiful mate at least part Fae but that she carried the healing gift as well. This was why Kheelan had taken her, and all of those humans before—he'd been searching for April.

Donovan's wolf snarled within him at the memory of that day. He'd only seen her for a brief moment, pressed his lips to hers just once, and then she was encouraging him to go save Jason. He'd been torn at the time, but the sound of Jason screaming was an excellent fucking motivator. When they returned a few short minutes later, after hearing her screams, their mate, their April was gone.

"Corrine!" Donovan was dragged from his musings by the roar of his Alpha. He shot a quick glance at Jason and then the two of them pushed their way through the crowd.

They pushed through to the front just in time to hear Corrine, a Fae Seer, and advisor to their Alpha, speak from where she was wrapped in Gabe's arms and held securely against his chest. "He brings her powers forward. He is fighting a strong incantation that has hidden her magic for many years, but he is forcing his way through the shields. She's scared, and in pain, but fighting him in her own way."

"She who?" Jason growled his voice more wolf than man.

Corrine turned to look at them, sadness shimmering in her eyes, and Donovan's heart seized in his chest. "Your mate."

Jason bellowed in rage, and his wolf exploded from him. Donovan's soul was making the same gut wrenching sound of pain, loss, and frustration, but he held strong to control his wolf. Just barely. Gabe was yelling something at Jason, but Donovan couldn't hear what he was saying over the roaring of his own blood in his ears.

Locking his gaze to the Fae seer, he asked the question he had been asking himself every minute of every hour since she'd been taken. "Where is she?"

Corrine reached out a hand and placed it on Donovan's arm. "If I knew, we would already be on our way, young wolf, but I do not know. All I can tell you is that you and your brother will play a role in helping her. You all have a long way to go before deciding her fate."

Donovan closed his eyes for a brief minute against the sense of hopelessness and relief that rolled through him. There was nothing worse for a dominant wolf like himself than knowing that the one person meant for him, the woman the fates had charged him with protecting, cherishing, and loving for the rest of his life, was in danger. They had no leads, no trail to follow, nothing that told them where she was, but hearing Corrine talk about her fighting and that they would all play a role in deciding her fate, meant that she was alive. This was the first damn time he'd had that reassurance, and the relief was almost enough to drop him to his knees.

When he opened his eyes and was able to focus on his surroundings, he realized the coronation was over, the Fae who had been invited to attend were shuffling out of the room, and Jason was trying to cover his dick with the shredded remains of his shirt. It was something Donovan would have found hilarious at one time, but with the wounds of Jason's torture visible as a clear reminder of what they had lost, he couldn't find the laughter in him. Hell, without April, he might never find it.

"We'll find her," he heard Erica say behind him. Donovan turned to face her. "She's strong. I only met her for a few minutes, but I could tell that straight away." Erica placed her hand on his arm, directly over a tattoo he'd had since it had come to him in a dream ten years ago. As soon as her hand touched the design, the world around him seemed to stop, and a moment later he felt a jolt rocket through him like he'd gripped onto a live wire and an image formed in his mind.

He saw a river running through a village, surrounded by mountains. A strange cluster of three tall stones that he recognized protruded from one of the ridges just outside the village. Beyond the village, further up the mountain, almost directly below the three tall stones, he saw a crevice in the cliff. The image began fading as that crevice came closer, and just as it faded, he caught sight of April. She ran out of the cliff face through that crevice, and the look on her face was a strange mixture of terror and determination. Her skin was streaked with dirt, tears had created tracks down her cheeks, and there was swelling along her left jaw. Her clothes were dirty, and her shirt had been ripped at her right shoulder. Then the image went dark.

Donovan's heart was pounding in his chest when he opened his eyes. The room was still frozen for a moment before returning to normal.

"We'll bring her home to you and Jason. That I promise you." Erica continued talking as if nothing had happened. With a startled look around the room, he realized that for her and every other person here, nothing had happened.

Still in shock, he simply nodded at the newly crowned queen of the Fae realm. Erica smiled then turned back to her mates. Donovan spun to look at Jason, who was pulling on a pair of jeans that one of the younger wolves in their pack had given him. "Did you just see something strange?"

Jason shot him a look. "Be more specific. "I've seen a lot of strange shit lately."

"No, like a vision or a dream, or fuck, I don't know … like some kind of foresight image or some shit like that."

Jason shook his head. "No."

Donovan's body began to vibrate with excitement. He knew that what he had seen was connected, the dream, the tattoo, the vision, everything. "Come on."

Jason frowned. "Where are we going?"

Donovan didn't pause as he strode out of the throne room, knowing that Jason was right on his heels. "I think it is about time we went and got our mate back. I know where to look. I've seen it, and I think she's managed to actually escape."

"What the ever loving fuck are you talking about?"

"I know where to find her."

"Should we tell Gabe?"

Donovan hesitated for a moment. His job as Beta was to protect his Alpha, and despite his recent actions, it was something he took great pride in. "No, this could be a trap. Just some magical hallucination Kheelan and his cronies have cooked up. We'll go alone, and if we find her, bring her back safe and sound."

"And if we find Kheelan?" Jason's voice had dropped to a deadly octave.

Donovan stopped and turned in the corridor to look his brother in the eye. "Then you get to rip out his heart, and hold it in front of him while it is still beating."

For the first time since he arrived in this realm, Donovan saw Jason smile. Sure it was bloodthirsty and filled with anticipation at the painful death of his tormentor, but it was a smile nonetheless.

Chapter Ten

"Heal me," Kheelan ordered her again.

"No!" April spat.

"Hurt her again," Kheelan commanded the other sadistic fuck, his sidekick, Frederych.

Not for the first time in the two weeks she'd been here, April felt her body convulse as if she were having a seizure. Frederych loomed over her with his hands—which never quite touched her body—as they roamed over her chest, then her belly, all the way down to her legs before coming back up again. At first, she would feel a mildly uncomfortable pulling sensation, but then it always escalated to something excruciatingly painful, as if his hands were magnets and her organs, her veins, her blood ... her magic, were all being drawn out of her body. At this point, her body would shake and buck uncontrollably and she would let out a blood-curdling scream, or at least she did for the first week. After that, she simply gritted her teeth and bore it, not wanting to give either of them the satisfaction.

At the highest peak of her pain, when she thought for sure that every internal part of her would be sucked out, twisting her insides out, a blue light would rise out of her and snap everything back into its place, throwing Frederych back against the wall. Kheelan had wisely learned to safeguard himself from this after the first time it happened and he, too, had been thrown.

"Heal me," Kheelan demanded again from the farthest corner of the room.

April was still reeling from the pain of having her insides settle back to normal when a maniacal laugh escaped her.

"What's so funny, bitch?"

"You're not looking so good there, Kheels," April

observed.

He'd been getting progressively worse every day since she'd been taken. His goon had managed to patch up the gaping hole in his stomach when they first brought her to this … secret lair—that was the best description she could come up with for the hovel they had brought her to. They had blindfolded and gagged her after entering the human realm and shoved her back into the same limo that had brought her and Jason to the woods the night all this horror had begun. At least it smelled like the same car, all old cigarette smoke and spilled alcohol.

April had been getting so sensitive to scent in the last couple of days. Things that she had never noticed before were suddenly logging in her memory.

****

Kheelan had torn off the blindfold and gag when they arrived at some strange looking cliff with three stones. Her demands about knowing what happened to her mates had fallen on deaf ears as Kheelan, Frederych, and two other guards had escorted her further up the mountain by foot until they reached a crevice in a cliff.

One of the goons had drawn a few symbols at the entrance before they all stepped in, and once again, just like when she had entered the Veil, April had felt a wave of nausea sweep over her. They must have entered another one of those portals, she figured.

She found herself in what she could only describe as a mad scientist's lab with otherworldly-looking machines and test tubes of various sizes filled with different colored liquids.

Kheelan had marched her straight into yet another cell with a hospital looking bed in the middle of the room. They had strapped her down and immediately began with her torture when she would not comply with

Kheelan's order to heal him.

After her blue shield, as she started to call it, tossed Frederych and Kheelan against the wall the first time, and they both recovered, she watched as Frederych put his hands over the hole in Kheelan's stomach. A black spark had emitted from his palms, and the hole closed up, leaving a giant scorch mark all around it. She had winced, seeing the redness and swelling that remained around the wound, which clearly indicated an infection. It was a temporary fix, she learned, one that the Fae had to administer to Kheelan daily, like a magical Band-Aid of sorts.

After one particularly torturous session, April had spat in Kheelan's face and said, "Even if I knew how to heal you, I still wouldn't do it. So go ahead and kill me, you bastard. I'll have the pleasure of knowing you'll be dying painfully soon after."

He had slapped her and stormed out of the room.

Later, he came back alone, only this time to torment her with his words. "You look so much like her ... your whore of a mother," he had sneered. Then his expression turned almost wistful. "Except for your coloring. Reysken had the most beautiful long red hair and the same big green eyes as you. He had far more freckles, however." He paused and seemed lost in his own memory. "They covered every damn inch of him."

Kheelan sounded like he actually cared about her father—if the man he spoke of was actually her father. Reysken, he had called him. April repeated the name in her mind several times, testing out the sound of it. Then the word "daddy" flashed in her mind, and she gasped. Kheelan just sneered again and continued his incessant descriptions of Reysken.

She suddenly found herself wanting to learn more about this man, but not from him, not from a man her father couldn't possibly have been in a relationship with, let alone been in love with, as Kheelan had declared.

"You are a liar, Kheelan," April had yelled in his face. "My father could never have been in love with someone like you. You're cruel and incapable of love."

"You have no idea, you filthy brat, of what I am capable." He'd leaned over her and got very close to her face. She wouldn't have thought it possible for his eyes to become colder. His lip then twisted in disgust. "I have loved two men in my life, both very deeply, and both of whom were honorable. You--you consort with filthy animals."

April had spat in Kheelan's face for the second time that day and braced herself for his assault. It didn't come this time, and it worried her even more. The bastard wasn't done with her yet.

"Hit a nerve, did I? I thought your father was honorable at first anyway. Until he met Ilyra. She bewitched him into thinking he was her mate, and he left me for her."

"That's not possible," April snapped. "You can't bewitch someone into thinking you are their mate. It's the most sacred, impenetrable bond there is."

"And how would you know this? You've been living among the humans."

"I've also lived with wolves, and I have seen firsthand the love and bond that forms between mates when I was with them, something you have clearly never experienced. But even I had no idea of its true power until I experienced it for myself."

Kheelan seemed unaffected by her remark. He smiled cruelly. "Your parents didn't get to experience it for very long."

April gritted her teeth. "What did you do to

them?"

"If your father had chosen me, if your father had trusted me, I would have only killed her. I would have even forgiven him for being part filthy beast since his Fae side was so dominant."

Was my father part shifter?

"I had no idea what he was," Kheelan continued. "Then I started hearing rumors about his dealings with a magician. I caught the mage training your mother and father on how to hide your filthy genes from the rest of our people. I couldn't believe he had hidden that part of himself from me for so long. I was furious. The mage was surprisingly easy to kill, but I admit, I hesitated with your father and underestimated how fiercely he would fight for his mate and child, which gave Ilyra the opportunity to escape with you."

The lights ... the blue lights from her palms ... cruel laughter ... her nightmares—they were echoes of her memories, ones that she had blocked out.

"I finally caught up with your mother a few days later. Sadly, she had already sent you away. She taunted me that I would never find you, so I ripped out her heart," Kheelan said dispassionately. "The whore obviously underestimated me, as I did indeed find you, didn't I?"

She had stared at Kheelan stony-faced, not wanting to give him the satisfaction of knowing he had gotten to her.

When he finally left the room, she'd broken down and allowed herself to cry freely, her sobs nearly choking her. Some of what he had said rang true, especially when this time she repeated her mother's name to herself. Then a memory of her parents flashed through her mind. A woman with blonde hair, blue eyes, and dimples in her cheeks, and a man with flowing red hair and bright green eyes were smiling as they tucked a five-year-old April into bed. They then walked out of her bedroom holding hands. The bittersweet memory only made her cry harder.

One way or another, Kheelan would suffer for what he did. She'd make damn sure of it.

Over and over, they'd tortured her, leaving only enough time in between for Frederych to recover from whatever toll it took on him to use his magic on her. During the brief breaks, she thought of her men, praying that Donovan had gotten to Jason in time and that they both had gotten away safely. Jason's screams still haunted her, but there was one moment when she closed her eyes and thought about the moment Jason had passionately kissed her in the diner, and the time Donovan had kissed her sweetly in her cell, that she fully felt that spark within her. She had touched it in her mind, cautiously at first, not knowing if this was yet another trick of Kheelan's to torture her.

The more she explored that part of herself, the more natural it had begun to feel to her and she became even surer that at least most of what she'd been told here was true. She was Fae. She was one of them ... a monster like Kheelan and his men. She was going to have to be as ruthless as these bastards if she was going to get out of this mess by using her powers against them.

By the next day, she had finally learned to reach inside of herself and draw out that spark of magic which until now had only manifested out of instinct. Believing it was actually there had been half the battle, and once April had admitted to herself that she was more than human, it was like a doorway had opened up inside her soul. Behind that door, she'd found the power she had been looking for.

****

When her tormenters arrived back in her cell, bright and early to begin their day's work of trying to coerce her to heal Kheelan, she was almost eager to see them this time—now that she had a plan. She was grateful that at least the awful sounding king was dead. More than once, she'd caught Kheelan blubbering about his former lover and how he longed to continue in his footsteps.

And now, as she laughed in Kheelan's face, tormenting *him* about his days being numbered, she reveled in that fact that soon he would be wiped off the face of the earth.

"I'd say you've got a week, maybe two tops, by the look of you, Kheels. I am so looking forward to your death."

"Again," he barked at Frederych, who had slowly just risen to his feet.

"But, Captain, I am not sure I ca—"

"I said again!"

This was it, her best chance, she thought. Frederych was truly the only one she feared, as Kheelan was still too weak to hurt her himself, and with him pretty much out of commission for the time being, she was ready for some payback.

"Please, no! I can't take anymore," she pleaded, hoping that they would believe her little scared act. As soon as the bastard reached her, she let loose her power, knocking both Kheelan and Frederych unconscious. She blasted through her restraints. Next, came the door. She would bring the whole goddamned place down if she had to, she thought as a murderous rage swept over her.

She remembered the direction they had brought her in and quickly made a run for it. Two guards stood at the entrance. She blasted one immediately, knocking him unconscious.

"I'll do worse to you if you don't open up the entry into the human realm."

Wide-eyed and clearly terrified, the Fae guard did as she asked. Then she blasted him anyway and launched herself into the human realm. She saw what looked to be a cluster of houses farther down the mountain and decided to make her way down there. She'd need to find a reason to explain why she looked so beat up and disheveled. She couldn't very well go telling tales of kidnapping Fae and wolves who shifted into men or she'd find herself locked up again in a different kind of cell.

Days spent in a dank dungeon, followed by two weeks in another less than sterile environment did not bode well for her appearance. Her clothes were dirty, her shirt torn, and she still felt the bruise on her face that Frederych had inflicted. The ones Kheelan had given her had already vanished due to her self-healing. She hadn't lied to him at first when she told him that she had no idea how'd she'd done it. It became second nature to her eventually, but she didn't understand why the wound Frederych had given her was healing at a slower rate than the damage Kheelan had inflicted. She couldn't quite put her finger on it, but there was something different about the other Fae.

April needed to come up with some excuses fast. Perhaps, she could simply say she got lost in the mountains. She quickly made her way down the rocky path and into the cover of the dense trees. She needed to get as much distance between herself and her captors as she could. There was no telling how long she had before they'd regain consciousness and come after her. After running full out for as long as her muscles could stand, she came across a flowing river, and her legs finally gave out.

She fell to her knees. Kheelan would come for her again. She knew it. And he'd hurt others, especially her men, to get to her. As much as she wanted to find them, to run into their arms, she had to stay away, at least until she was certain that Kheelan was dead. She would rather die herself than allow that vile Fae scum to ever harm her men again.

She put her head in her hands and cried, knowing she may never see her mates again. She needed to rest, just for a moment, so she hid under the branches of a bush next to the flowing water and closed her eyes.

"April!"

She woke suddenly when she heard a familiar voice calling out to her.

Jason.

Oh my God, how long was I asleep?

She lifted her head to see Donovan, followed by Jason, running toward her. She then crawled out of her not so hidey-hole and stood on shaky legs, trying to convince herself that she had to run in the other direction. Her traitorous legs, exhausted as she was, ran to them instead, and she launched herself into Donovan's arms. Jason caught up and hugged her from behind.

"I thought I'd never see you again," Jason fervently whispered in her ear, relief at having her in his arms clearly evident in his tone. "I'm never letting you out of my sight again."

"Me either," Donovan echoed just as passionately. "I've barely even had the chance to have you *in* my sight. Do they know that you're missing?"

April nodded into his chest. *At least they will when they regain consciousness if they haven't already.*

"Let's get going then," Donovan said, prompting them to pull apart from their embrace. He cupped her cheeks and gently traced the bruise on her jaw. He looked murderous as did Jason who came to stand in front of her as well. "How badly are you hurt, angel?"

"Just pick her up and carry her," Jason said impatiently, "before I go up that mountain and tear apart every single one of those fuckers now.

"Patience, brother. We'll come back and do recon, but we need to get April somewhere safe first."

"No," she whispered, her voice shaky.

"What?" Donovan asked, surprised, his brows furrowing in confusion. "As much as I want to rip them apart along with my brother, I am not risking your safety and we need to make sure to be prepa—"

"I meant, no, I am not going with you two," she replied more firmly.

"Excuse me?" Jason asked. "What the hell do you mean you're not going with us? Did we not just make it clear to you that we are not letting you out of our sight again?"

"Don't you see?" she cried out, startling them both. She held her hands out, palms facing forward and let her blue spark gently fizzle out of them. "I am what Kheelan said. Fae. A monster just like *them*. He hurt you because of me," she continued, tears pouring down her face. "I don't deserve to be your mate, and I won't let him hurt you again."

Jason got right in her face. "Are you done now?" he asked matter-of-factly.

She opened her mouth to speak, but he turned his back on her.

"Let's go," he said walking away.

Before she even had time to ponder if that meant they were going to listen to her and leave without her, Donovan scooped her up and threw her over his shoulder and then he and Jason made a run for it.

Chapter Eleven

"We're home," Donovan exclaimed when they pulled up to a cozy-looking ranch style cabin surrounded by deep lush woods. His words had been the first ones spoken since they carried her off, caveman style.

"I already have a home," April muttered before stepping out of the car.

"It's not safe for you there, angel."

"Regardless of whether or not it's safe for her," Jason interrupted, looking none too pleased with her comment, "her place is with us." He stormed off ahead and opened the door to the cabin.

"I'm filthy," April said once they were all inside and Donovan had closed the door behind them.

"April, you are not filthy." It was Donovan's turn to be displeased now. "Listen, we need to talk about what hap—"

"I meant I haven't showered in over two weeks," she said quietly. Both Donovan and Jason looked at her with pained expressions. It was glaringly obvious that the lack of bathing was the least of their concern of what had been done to her.

Donovan held his hand out to her. "Come. The shower's this way." He jutted his chin in the direction of the hallway.

"I think I can find it on my own. Unless you mean to carry me again?" She gave them both a pointed look.

Jason stepped forward, but Donovan placed a hand on his chest, halting his movement. "Use the one in the master bedroom. It's bigger."

April nodded and walked off.

"Just give her some time, brother," she heard

Donovan whisper to Jason. "We have no idea what that bastard did to her yet."

The rest of their conversation was cut off to her recently overly sensitive ears when she finally reached the en suite bathroom and shut the door. She threw her clothes in the trashcan by the sink, making a mental note to burn them later. Her nightmares of being held captive would be reminder enough of what she had gone through at the hands of Kheelan. She certainly did not need the clothes she wore as a second reminder.

The spray of the hot water soothed her aching muscles, and as she stood there, washing away the dirt and grime that had accumulated on her body, a sudden pang of guilt set in. She realized she had been unfair, cruel even, to Donovan and Jason. They came for her, would have found her if she hadn't escaped, and all she did was push them away and snipe at them. She felt even less deserving of them now, and she wondered how they could still possibly want her after what she had revealed to them earlier.

She grabbed the nearest towel and dried herself off and realized that she had no clothes to put on. Fortunately, she spied an oversized sweatshirt hanging on one of the hooks and put it on. She inhaled deeply, immediately recognizing the owner's delicious musky scent. Donovan. She also knew that the woodsy-scented towel she had just used belonged to Jason.

She felt a sudden twinge of longing and desire for her two men and allowed herself one fleeting moment of hope that Jason would forgive her for what was done to him because of her and that Donovan would forgive her as well for what was done to his brother. The moment passed, and self-hatred along with doubt took the place of hope. How could they possibly forgive her when she could not forgive herself?

When she stepped out of the bathroom, Donovan and Jason were waiting for her in the bedroom. Donovan sat at the edge of the king-sized bed while Jason looked at her from the armchair next to it. She didn't miss the fact that they both ogled her bare legs as she stepped closer to them. She felt her entire body heat up from the intensity of their stares.

"I like the way my shirt looks on you, angel." Donovan's voice was low and husky. He got up suddenly from the bed to stand in front of her. "Talk to us, April. Please."

"How could the two of you still possibly want me?" April's words came out rushed and strangled. She closed her eyes, swallowing the rest of the speech she had prepared for them as if her vocal cords stubbornly refused to say goodbye to them.

"Cut that shit out, April," Jason bellowed before he, too, stood before her. She flinched at the harshness of his tone. "I'm the one who failed you. Not the other way around."

"How can you say that? It was me Kheelan was after all this time. Not you. He took Dee and God knows how many others, all to get to me. Oh God, Dee! Have they found her yet?"

"No," Donovan said quietly. "But we will. I swear it."

"He'll just keep coming for me." She reached out and placed her hand on Jason's cheek. "I felt so helpless when you were in that cell. I can't bear the thought of him hurting you like that again." She turned to Donovan and put her other hand on his cheek. "And it's not only Jason's screams I dreamt about. Sometimes it was you I pictured Kheelan torturing. I'd rather die than to ever let him get his hands on either of you. Not when I can prevent it." She took a deep steady breath. Her words would not fail her this time. "You both have to let me go."

"Fuck that!" Jason growled. Before she even had time to blink, she found herself tossed on the bed. Her hands were held above her head by Donovan while Jason fiercely, unyieldingly took her mouth in a fiery kiss. She returned it with the same fervor, unable to help herself.

April had no time to think, to collect her thoughts, for as soon as Jason released her lips, Donovan took his place. He released the grip he had on her wrists, but instead of pushing him away, she wrapped her hands around his neck and pulled him closer to her. She'd only had a brief taste of him when he came to rescue her from the dungeons, so this felt like their first real kiss. She found her resolve quickly fading because she sensed their pain at the thought of her leaving them. She knew she didn't have the strength to walk away from them on her own, and it seemed that neither of her stubborn men was willing to let her go.

When Donovan ended their kiss, he looked deeply into her eyes and cradled her face. Like that first night with Jason, she felt as if he could see the inside of her soul. He wasn't repulsed by her or angry. Instead, he looked at her with longing and adoration.

"That's not the way this works, my angel. Whatever happens to one of us, happens to all three."

"And we would chase you to the ends of the Earth, April," Jason added. "So don't even think about running from us."

She felt hope flaring inside of her once again. She understood now. She would never stop fighting for Donovan and Jason either. She remembered Jason telling her in the limo that he didn't care what or who she was, but still, she had to be sure. "You don't care that I am Fae like Kheelan?"

"Not all Fae are monsters," Donovan replied. "Just like not all shifters are good. You had the misfortune of meeting some pretty nasty ones, but I believe you also met Erica."

"Who?" Then it hit her. "The woman in the dungeons with me?"

Donovan nodded. "A healer, like you, something very rare and sought after amongst the Fae. She's also the True Queen and now sits on the Fae throne, and she is one of the strongest, bravest women I know, second to you. She and her mates were gracious enough to forgive me for what I did to them. So was Jason."

"What did you do?"

Donovan explained how he had assisted Erica in her cause to face Aelfric alone, once again because of Kheelan, who had threatened to kill her and Jason and left Donovan with very little choice. April wasn't the least bit surprised that Donovan did the right thing immediately after, and she couldn't blame him for his choice. She saw him as nothing less than a brave man, who loved and protected fiercely. She told him so.

"Thank you, angel."

"You give me too much credit, brother," Jason said. "I'm not sure I *wouldn't* have done the same thing as you."

"I want him to hurt so badly," April said through gritted teeth. "He murdered my parents, and he and my father…"

Maybe there had been something good in Kheelan once if her father had loved him, but she could see nothing but darkness in his soul as he stood looming above her, delighting in her pain.

"Tell us what happened, April," Jason gently

prodded.

She nodded. Jason and Donovan were her mates. They deserved to know it all, so she told them everything he had done to her, how he and Frederych had tried to pull her powers from her. They both tried to hide their pained expressions, but she saw them and instantly regretted telling them that part. She moved on to the conversation she had had with Kheelan about what she had learned about her parents, including the fact that she possessed some wolf genes. She swatted them away as they both surreptitiously tried to sniff her during her storytelling. Throughout all of it, though, she only saw compassion in their eyes for what she had lost and anger at how she had suffered—or perhaps it was more like murderous rage.

In any case, it made her feel closer to Jason and Donovan, free, with no secrets left between them. She knew who she was now and so did they, but none of it mattered or changed the fact that they belonged to each other.

After she had told them her story, they had all just quietly lay together, her snuggled in between Jason and Donovan, but after a little while of silent reflection, something in the air had changed. An undeniable electric charge had started to pulse between April and her men.

"Let us show you how much we want you, angel." Donovan nuzzled her ear as he spoke.

"Yes," she whispered, closing her eyes, prompting Donovan to continue with his assault on her ear. He licked her inner shell then proceeded to torment her ear with soft bites and kisses, eliciting a few successive moans from her. He moved onto to delivering the same attention to her neck while Jason's warm hands caressed her bare legs.

Donovan cupped her face. She opened up her

eyes for a brief moment and saw him hovering over her. His lips quirked in an adorable sly smile before he pressed them to hers. He kissed her softly at first, their tongues barely touching, but when she hugged him to her tightly, he deepened the kiss, moaning into her mouth. His hand cupped her breast over the thick sweatshirt, but she felt it searing into her skin as if she had been wearing nothing at all.

She felt Jason shift in between her legs. His hands roamed up her thighs, and under her shirt, stopping at her hips. He placed his forehead on her lower stomach. "Do you have any idea how difficult it has been lying here, not touching you, knowing you had nothing underneath this sweatshirt?" His voice, muffled by said shirt, sounded strained.

Donovan hummed in agreement and moved on to kissing her neck. She nudged him a little so that he could give her room to sit up. She then lifted her hands in the air. It didn't take long for them to catch her meaning. Donovan peeled off the sweatshirt from her body, slowly revealing every naked inch of her to their gaze.

Jason pulled her to him and kissed her deeply. He cupped her ass and brought her flush against his body. She felt his hard cock against her skin and ached for him to put it inside her.

"You're breathtaking," he murmured against her lips right before he laid her back down on the bed with him on top of her.

"Isn't she, brother?" Donovan lifted up her hand to kiss the inside of her wrist as Jason trailed kisses along her jawline, down to her neck and chest.

April panted heavily as he continued kissing and licking down her body. His warm hands cupped her breasts as he kissed in between them. Then he sucked her nipples into his mouth in turn before continuing his downward path.

She turned her head to see Donovan remove his shirt, revealing a solid muscular chest with rock hard abs. She made a mental note to ask him about his uniquely stunning tribal tattoo, but now all she wanted were his hands touching her as well. As if sensing her desire, he leaned into her for a kiss while his hands roamed her breasts and stomach.

He then moved back to kissing and licking her ear. "I'm going to memorize each and every one of your freckles and play connect the dots with my tongue," he whispered in her ear causing her to giggle, not just from his words, but from the sensation of feeling his warm breath on one hell of an erogenous zone.

Her laughter cut off immediately when Jason's lips connected with her clit. He sucked it into his mouth, his hand pressing against her flat stomach to keep her from bucking, and she threw her head back, releasing a loud moan. Donovan took advantage of her exposed neck and alternated kissing and sucking every inch of it, while his wicked hands massaged her breasts and plucked her nipples.

April lifted her hands over her head to grasp the pillow as Donovan kissed a path down her neck all the way to her breasts and Jason continued to lick and suck on her clit. When he added two fingers into her core and expertly massaged her inner walls, she lost it. She opened her mouth in a silent scream as an earth shattering orgasm ripped through her body. Both Donovan and Jason continued to drive her wild, quickly building her up again. When she felt her second climax closing in on her, they stopped.

They didn't leave her bereft of their touch for long, however. Donovan stripped off his jeans, revealing the fact that he had gone commando. His long thick cock stood at attention, his thick mushroomed head purple. April licked her lips.

"Not now, angel. I need to be inside you."

Jason shifted on the bed to make room for Donovan between her legs. He kissed her sweetly on the cheek before lying down next to her. Donovan spread her legs and massaged her thighs as he looked at her. "We're going to show you who you belong to. We're going to make you ours."

And then he plunged inside of her to the hilt. April gasped at the sensation of being completely filled by him.

"You okay?" he asked, his voice straining.

"Yes … oh please, don't stop. You feel so fucking good."

Donovan looked pleased with her declaration and pulled almost all the way out and then slammed back into her. April fisted the pillow tighter and moaned successively as he plunged in and out of her. He lowered himself completely flush on top of her and entwined his hands with hers as he continued to rock into her. She wrapped her legs around his hips to feel him even deeper, and then she lifted her head up slightly so that she could kiss his lips. Soft kisses turned into fervent ones as their tongues entwined. Donovan growled low in the back of his throat when she gently bit down on his lip.

"Oh God," she moaned when he did the same to her. She felt her muscles spasm and contract, making him feel snugger inside her.

"Fuck, baby," he roared in reaction.

"Agh! What…" Not only was she on the precipice of coming again, but she felt that familiar tingling in her gums like the night she and Jason were at the diner. "I need…" Her incisors lowered, and she felt a strong urge to sink them into Donovan's neck.

"Don't be afraid," she heard Jason say next to her.

"Do it, angel," Donovan uttered, his voice unsteady. She knew he was close, too.

Losing any semblance of control she didn't even know why she held onto, April let her baser instincts take over. She sank her teeth into Donovan's neck and swallowed the salty coppery taste of his blood, surprisingly enjoying the flavor. She felt Donovan's sharp teeth sink into the soft fleshy part of her neck where it met the shoulder. She unclamped her teeth from Donovan and screamed out her release just as he roared his. Her body continued to spasm for what felt like an eternity. He held onto her tightly, their hands and bodies entwined, until the last remnants of her orgasm were wrung out.

Finally, when she was able to breathe normally again, Donovan delivered several soft kisses to her lips. She had no words for what she had just experienced. She felt even more connected to him now than before, and the emotion of it nearly choked her.

"It's okay," Donovan whispered, wiping away a tear that had just escaped her. He then buried his head in her neck and gave her one final squeeze before pulling out of her and shifting over to her other side.

"Jason," she whispered, turning to look at him. "I need you, too. Please."

He hesitated for a moment, confusing her. When he sat up and then removed his shirt, she understood the reason for his hesitation.

"Oh my God, Jason." April reached out to touch the scars that should have healed by now, making him flinch. "I don't understand."

"Kheelan used some kind of poisoned tipped

knife on me. Erica tried, but…" Jason looked away from her, as if ashamed, but April was having none of it.

She sat up in front of him and touched his scars again. He still would not look at her, and she watched him grit his teeth as her hands roamed over the several slashes on his stomach. She channeled her abilities now that she knew how and focused. After a few seconds, she gasped. She found the poison, could touch it with her mind, but when she tried to grab onto to it to remove it, she discovered something shocking.

"You're holding onto them as a reminder. Why, Jason?"

He finally looked at her, confusion evident on his face. Donovan had sat up as well, probably wanting an explanation, too.

"I don't … I didn't realize." He lowered his head. "I failed to keep you safe, baby. I deserve these scars."

"Fuck that!" April spat, mimicking Jason's own words from earlier. "Look at me," she snapped when he continued to look down at the bed. When he finally lifted his head, she took Jason's hand and placed it against her heart. "You didn't deserve any of it. You and Donovan fought for me, and I know you always will. Please let your guilt go. For me."

With his free hand, Jason wiped away her tears. "I knew you'd turn out to be a little firecracker." He pulled her close to him and kissed her softly, and April took advantage of his openness by finding the darkness lurking deep inside of him and blasting it out of existence.

When they pulled apart from their kiss, Jason's scars were gone.

Chapter Twelve

Jason was shocked as April ran her fingers over his now smooth skin. He had to finally admit to himself that he had indeed been punishing himself by holding onto the scars as a reminder of his failure, whether consciously or not. It had been a blow to his pride how utterly he'd failed April when they'd first met, but if she had forgiven him, then the least he could do was spend the rest of his life proving to her that he could and would do better as her mate.

"Hey," April pulled his face around so she could look into his eyes, "why so serious? I want to celebrate being with my mates at last. We can't change the past, Jason, but we can move forward."

"You're right, babe." A slow, sexy smile replaced the frown on his lips. "And I really *do* want to move forward."

April's laugh, as he waggled his eyebrows in a suggestive manner, was exactly what he was aiming for. Now should be a time of celebration, and he wanted to celebrate with his mate over and over again until all three of them could no longer move. He stood and removed his pants, then crawled onto the bed in front of April. Jason loved how her breathing grew choppy and her eyes clouded in desire when she saw his hard cock weeping to be inside of her.

"Are you ready for me, love?" Jason moved closer until he was on his knees in front of her.

He groaned when she bit her lip and nodded at him. She then reached out to touch him once again. Jason sat back on his heels and pulled her in close to him, urging her to wrap her legs around his hips until she was perched straddling his lap. Goddess, he could feel the heat of her pussy where it now rested over his cock. He moved her hips back and forth ever so slightly, loving how wet she was for him.

"I want to watch your face for every second of this, April," he said looking straight into her eyes. "I want to see into your very soul when I'm inside of you."

"Please, Jason … I need you."

He took her mouth in a slow and thorough kiss, pouring into it every emotion he'd had since the night he'd met her in the bar. Excitement, hope, lust, fear, grief, it was all there, and he wanted her to feel how much he needed her. How much *they* needed her to complete their lives.

Jason moved one hand around to delve between the lush and swollen lips between her legs, and he couldn't stop the moan that came from deep within him as her honey soaked his fingers. He felt Donovan move up behind her, and April gasped into his mouth as his brothers' hands came around and covered her breasts.

"Oh God, yes," she moaned, her hips bucking in his grip when his thumb found her swollen clit and tapped it a few times before he slid two fingers deep inside of her.

Jason pulled back from his assault on her mouth and looked at her, their perfect mate, her head leaning back, eyes closed in rapture as Donovan nipped and sucked at her neck and shoulder.

"Open your eyes, baby. Look at me."

April opened her beautiful green eyes and smiled at him. She was seduction personified, her lips flushed and swollen from their kisses, her pale skin a contrast against their tanned arms. Her long red hair was loose, falling around her shoulders, making her look like the fairy seductress from folk tales who would lead any man to his ruin.

Jason was still astonished that the Goddess saw fit to give them a mate so extraordinary as April, and he said a silent prayer to her in thanks as he smiled back at April. When he moved his aching cock to notch at her entrance and slowly moved forward, he was thankful for his enhanced sight so he could take in everything about her as he pushed inside of her for the first time. How her eyes dilated wider with the pleasure, how her breath caught in her chest, and when she bit her bottom lip once again, he couldn't hold out any longer. He thrust into her until he was completely surrounded by her decadent heat.

"Goddess, you feel amazing, love." He panted as he tried to control his thrusts. "No one has ever felt as right as you do."

"Jason, please," she answered as Donovan continued to caress her breasts and kiss her neck and shoulders. "I need to come so badly."

"Donovan, why don't we give our mate a taste of what she really needs?" Jason looked over at his brother and smiled. When one of Donovan's hands moved from her breast he quickly replaced it with his own. Jason knew the exact second that his brother's finger breached April's ass because he could feel her spasm around his cock and he saw her eyes grow wide in surprise.

"Soon, baby, you will feel what it's like to have us both in you at the same time. I promise you're going to love it."

"Oh yes," she moaned as her hips began to thrash and buck. "Harder … please!"

He released the last of his control and began to thrust into her with everything he had. Jason knew he wouldn't last much longer, so when he pinched her clit between his fingers and felt her tense as her orgasm flooded throughout her entire body, he let himself come as well. He leaned forward to sink his teeth into the most beautiful woman in the world.

He felt her sharp teeth pierce his own skin, and for the first time in what seemed like forever, Jason felt whole as the mate bond cemented into place among all three of them.

He was still panting, holding April close to him when he noticed that Donovan had gotten up and gone to the bathroom, returning with a warm washcloth to see to their mate. April's sleepy smile as Jason pulled back the covers and tucked her under the sheets, had his wolf almost more content than when he'd claimed her. They were meant to take care of this lovely creature. This was what they'd been born to do.

"Come here, you two. I want to feel you against me as I bask in the after bliss," she teased, pulling them down on each side of her to cuddle against her. "That was amazing by the way."

"It will only get better, angel," Donovan whispered in her ear as he pulled the covers up over her.

"Seriously, I can barely form words. If it gets better than that, I may lose consciousness."

"Don't worry, love, we'll still make sure you enjoy it." Jason winked at her before he nuzzled into her shoulder after he laid his head on the pillow next to hers.

Suddenly April gasped. Jason opened his eyes to see a peculiar look on her face.

"April? What's wrong?" Donovan asked, sounding as panicked as Jason felt.

She sat up, pushed the covers away, moved to the end of the bed, and held her arms out in front of her, indicating they should give her some space.

"I don't … know. Something feels odd inside of me." She rubbed her hands along her arms. "It's like a million tiny needles on the inside of my skin. Not painful

… exactly, but …oh my God!"

Jason panicked when she scrambled off the bed, dragging the comforter with her, and landed with a loud thump on the floor. He and Donovan swiftly moved toward the foot of the bed, ignoring her pleas not to look at her.

"Please, please, just give me a minute," she cried out desperately.

They both sat back, looking at each other in confusion. Jason tried not to panic, thinking perhaps it could be a female thing, but when he heard her moan and it abruptly turned into a high pitched whimper, Jason and Donovan dove off the bed. Jason's eyes widened at the sight before him amongst the now tattered comforter.

An astonishingly beautiful wolf with reddish fur sat shaking where their mate had just been.

Chapter Thirteen

"Holy fuck! You shifted into a wolf," Jason shouted, pointing at where April's wolf cowered on the bedroom floor. He then lifted his gaze to Donovan's, the shock clear on his face. "She shifted into a wolf!"

"I can see that, Captain Obvious, thank you!" Donovan snapped back before turning his worried gaze to their mate. Moving as slowly as he could, Donovan crouched low on the floor, making sure to give her as much room as possible, not wanting to add to her fear and anxiety.

"April." He let all the awe he felt for his mate show in his tone. "Your wolf is so damn beautiful. Apparently your wolf genes aren't so latent after all."

She lifted her muzzle from the floor a couple of inches until she could meet Donovan's eyes, her gaze seemingly assessing his reaction.

Keeping his expression as open as he could, he reached out toward her. "You're a red wolf, baby, which is not surprising considering all those red curls of yours. Your fur," he added, gently sweeping his hand into her fur, loving the texture of it between his fingers, "is a beautiful mixture of red, with subtle hints brown and gold."

Donovan smiled as he ran his eyes over the wolf that looked quizzically up at him. "You have this dark black tipped tail that is so damn cute."

Her eyes narrowed, and a growl burst forth only to be cut off short. Her eyes widened in shock.

"Yeah, beautiful," Jason murmured as he joined them both on the floor, stroking a hand down April's flank. "That's your wolf telling Donovan she's not cute. She is badass, which totally makes sense considering who you are." Jason nudged her gently, and April moved around so that she was sitting on her hindquarters in front of them, and Donovan shifted to mirror Jason's position, sitting with his back against the bed.

"I have no idea what the hell is going on," Donovan admitted. "I have no idea why we couldn't scent your wolf, but there is something that we need to do, love. We have claimed you as men, and tonight has been the best fucking night of my life."

"Mine too," Jason agreed.

"Can our wolves meet yours, angel?" Donovan sensed her apprehension and rushed to reassure her. "She is already theirs. Our mating has cemented that. Search within her, and she will tell you that she wants to meet her wolves just as much as you wanted to be with your men. Please."

Donovan's wolf paced within him, impatience in every step and twitch of his tail. He could scent his mate, and he wanted out. After a moment's of hesitation, the red wolf nodded slowly, and Donovan released the breath he had been holding. He shared a quick glance with his brother, a look he hoped said "take this slow or I'll kill you", and let his wolf take over.

Within a moment, he and Jason had shifted. He now welcomed the slight pain it took to bring forth his wolf and knew that April would learn to do the same. He and Jason were dominant wolves. Perhaps he should have warned her that there would be an immediate urge to submit to them. April's wolf whined in confusion before she finally stopped fighting and submitted to him.

It shouldn't have been such a surprise that their mate's animal half was so strong. Her human personality was not used to submitting to those around her, but her wolf would show her the way. The knowledge that this beautiful, strong woman and wolf was his had him filling with pride. He stepped forward and buried his nose into April's neck, rumbling low in his chest as her scent filled his lungs. She carried the wild, earthy scent of her wolf and the citrusy deliciousness of their April. Very gently, he opened his jaws and bit her on the back of her neck. The wolf beneath him froze.

He held still for a moment and then stepped back, allowing Jason's wolf the opportunity to step forward and complete the ritual as well. After Jason's wolf bit April's, he stepped back and waited, watching her for a moment. April stepped forward hesitantly, burying her nose in Jason's neck as if familiarizing herself with his scent, before mimicking their moves of moments before and sinking her teeth into him.

When she turned her eyes on Donovan, his wolf tensed. His wolf was more dominant than Jason's, and most wolves in general, which was why he was Beta. He held himself still as she stepped forward and pressed her nose to his neck. His wolf growled low, and April tensed. But by the Gods, he was hers.

With a wolfy chuff, one that Donovan could only describe as glee, April stepped forward and bit down gently on Donovan's neck. A wave of emotions swept over him, nearly overwhelming all of his senses.

Donovan urgently needed to feel her in his arms. This moment was more than he had ever dreamed, more than he could ever have imagined, but right now he needed to hold his mate. He pushed forward, driving his grumbling wolf to the background as he embraced his human side. Jason followed suit, and the two of them knelt on the floor in their human forms.

April looked between him and Jason. Donovan could see panic start to settle in her eyes.

"Do you want to change back, baby?" When she

nodded enthusiastically he smiled gently. "All you have to do is think about your human self. Close your eyes and let your wolf go. She won't be gone for good. She'll simply drop back within you. There will be some discomfort in the shift that you need to prepare for, but soon it will be quick and natural for you to let her out."

The beautiful wolf before him closed her eyes. After a shimmer of energy, which Donovan had never before truly appreciated, April was back in her human form, and staring at them with her startling green eyes.

"Am I okay?" she whispered, a tremble in her voice that had Donovan's chest aching for her.

"More than just okay," he whispered back, reaching out and pulling her onto his lap.

Jason pulled her legs up to lay them across his thighs. "You are fucking amazing. You are a Fae healer, rare and exquisite, and just as astounding, you're a wolf shifter as well."

"How can this be? I can actually feel her inside me now, but I have never sensed her before. Do you think that this has anything to do with what Kheelan did to me?" April sounded panicked, her voice catching on the last word. Donovan squeezed her against his chest.

If she cried, he might just put his own head back and howl, too. "I don't know, baby, but we'll find out. I don't think it's possible to create a wolf shifter and you do have wolf genes, but we can go to Corrine and Erica and ask them if they know why you never felt yours before."

"And if they don't know," Jason continued, "then we will go back across the Veil and track some fucker down who does know. That might actually be Kheelan, and I owe him a beating and a view of his own beating heart, so I am okay with that scenario."

April laughed softly, sniffing delicately, and

Donovan knew she had been closer to tears than he realized. "You know, I am okay with that, too. But let's start with this Corrine person and Erica first, huh?"

April was quiet for a moment, and Donovan was happy to simply hold her. After a moment, she shifted on his lap so she could look into his eyes.

"In all the excitement, I never did ask you how you two found me."

Donovan lifted a hand to sweep a lock of her beautiful red hair from her forehead. "Ten years ago, I had this dream. This woman with blonde hair and blue eyes held her finger above the skin on my arm and drew an image. She never actually touched me, but to me, it felt like she was literally carving it into my arm. I had never felt pain in a dream before, but in that moment, it burned like a son of a bitch. She uttered some words, that to this day I have no idea what language she used, but it sounded like a chant or something like that. When she was finished, the image shone brightly on my skin. She looked me in the eye and told me that I had to get the image tattooed exactly as she drew it and in the same spot. The dream was so damn vivid that as soon as I awoke, I sketched the image and took it to someone who could do it justice. She never told me why it was so important. She simply told me that it must be done and that one day it would show me my reason for living."

Donovan laughed as those words suddenly made sense. "And it did. That tattoo led us straight to you. Erica touched my arm at her coronation, and as soon as she did, I got this clear image of where you were being held. Maybe she activated it somehow without realizing."

April sighed and snuggled closer. "That's cool."

He and Jason both chuckled at their mate's easy acceptance of something that would normally register quite high on someone's weird shit-o-meter.

Donovan was about to suggest that they climb right back into the bed because his dick was starting to get ideas with her soft ass pressed against it so deliciously, but he was interrupted by the familiar opening of Metallica's "Master of Puppets".

"Shit!" he groaned as he laid his head back against the bed. He cast a quick glance at his brother, who looked a little sick himself. Their Alpha was calling. Donovan had picked that song for his ringtone because he considered it to be fairly apt for Gabe.

"Master of Puppets?" April asked looking over her shoulder at his phone vibrating atop the bedside table.

Donovan's jaw dropped as his mate amazed him yet again. It was just his luck that he found the perfect woman who could kick ass, heal an injury, fight for everything she believed in, and to top it all off, knew the opening strains of one of the best guitar riffs of any song in the world as far as he was concerned, on the day his Alpha finally killed him.

Karma really was a bitch.

****

"Gabe, he's bleeding on the carpet! How many times have I told you to try to keep the boys in the ring?"

Corrine's voice rang through the downstairs gym in Gabe's house, and Donovan groaned as he turned his head to look towards her. She was standing on the bottom stair, opposite side of the gym to where he lay, with both hands on her hips, glaring at the man who had just thrown him over the ropes of the boxing ring and into the wall. He struggled to draw breath as he lay on the aforementioned carpet. And he was most definitely bleeding. Donovan took it as a good sign that he was actually conscious, because, for all intents and purposes, he shouldn't be.

"Don't blame me," Gabe grunted from where he stood in the ring, hands on his own hips, his eyes still blazing with anger. "He should have gotten up quicker."

"Oh, my God!" April shrieked from behind Corrine and scampered over toward Donovan.

Donovan groaned again at the fact that his mate was seeing him like this. He had hoped that she would have stayed upstairs, safe and unaware of this beating, but he should have known better. When they had first arrived, he and Jason had both kissed her with a type of desperation before they left her with Corrine. Not because they thought that Gabe would actually kill them—well, Donovan was fairly certain he wouldn't, maybe—but because they didn't think they would be able to kiss her without pain after the meeting Gabe had insisted they have. And by a meeting he meant ass-kicking in the boxing ring downstairs in the gym.

"What the hell is wrong with you?" April growled at Gabe as she pulled Donovan's head onto her lap. Donovan figured while he was there, Gabe couldn't beat on him for not calling and letting him know what was going on anymore. Win-win as far as he was concerned.

"Damn, Gabe," Jason moaned in a pain-filled voice as he stood up from the other side of the ring, blood dripping profusely from his nose, his arm wrapped around his ribs that no doubt hurt as much as Donovan's did. "You hit with the force of a fucking freight train."

April gasped as she looked up over at Jason, and Donovan felt her tense beneath his head. A low continuous growl erupted from her chest, and from the change in her scent, Donovan knew her wolf was about to put in an appearance. When their mate had shifted back to her skin at their house, the scent of her wolf had faded away to nothing, but now, with her wolf riding close to the surface, her scent changed. Before he could issue a warning, April's wolf burst from her with a snarl. Corrine's gasp could be heard from where she remained by the stairs.

"What the ever-loving fuck is going on here?" Gabe asked, shock clearing his face of all the anger that had filled it just moments before. "I thought she was Fae?"

Donovan pushed himself up to a seated position, pressing a hand against his ribs that moved underneath his touch, alerting him to the fact that they were broken and not just cracked. "That's what I wanted to tell you at the beginning, but you wouldn't let me get a fucking word in edgewise."

April's wolf, still snarling and growling, was edging its way toward the boxing ring and more importantly, toward her prey … Gabe. Biting back a groan of pain, Donovan got to his feet, desperately trying to think of a way to stop what was about to happen.

April's wolf leaped nimbly into the ring, and Gabe grinned, his wolf clear in his eyes as he stared the approaching wolf down. "You're an aggressive little thing, aren't you? But there is something little wolves like you need to learn really fucking fast. There is always a bigger, badder, and meaner wolf in the woods than you, but there is no wolf bigger, badder, and meaner than me."

Gabe's wolf burst from him in a shift so fast it occurred in the blink of an eye. His pure black wolf, more than twice the size of April's, had more dominance in him than anything Donovan had ever encountered. Gabe snarled back at April, and his dominance filled the room, dropping him and Jason to their knees and April onto her belly with a pained whimper.

Corrine, the only one in the room unaffected by

Gabe's display of dominance, stomped towards the boxing ring.

"Oh good grief, Gabe," Corrine rolled her eyes. "This poor woman has been through enough, and you have made your two pack mates pay for being dumbasses and not coming to you before they rode off like white knights to get to their mate. Stop being a dominant asshole and let them up. I think there are a couple of questions that need to be asked, and I for one am not sure if we have all the answers."

Gabe's wolf looked at Corrine, acceding to her wishes, and then both he and Corrine left the room.

Chapter Fourteen

April closely watched Gabe's wolf as he trotted off after Corrine. Once they disappeared up the stairs, her wolf ascertained that her mates were finally safe and the need to protect them—even from their own Alpha, subsided. She looked at her two bloodied mates, who both sported equally goofy and perhaps somewhat lopsided grins, considering the fact that their faces were slightly *rearranged*. She then growled at *them*. What the hell did they find so amusing anyway, she wondered. If they hadn't been wolf shifters, they'd both be rushed to a hospital by now, dealing with multiple broken bones and lacerations, and more than likely some internal bleeding.

"It's okay, love," Jason reassured. "It looks much worse than it is."

"We'll be fine in a few hours," Donovan added with a wince.

A few hours my ass! She was a healer after all, and no way would she let her mates hurt for a few more hours. April shifted easily this time. Her worry for Jason and Donovan were something that she and her wolf agreed upon.

"Let me heal you," she ordered sternly.

"Isn't she amazing?" Jason asked Donovan without taking his eyes off her.

"Absolutely perfect," Donovan replied with the same amount of wonder in his tone. Then both men began to strip out of their clothing.

"Hey," she snapped, "I highly doubt this is the appropriate time for sex considering your extensive injuries, not to mention the fact that we are in your asshole boss's house and—"

Both Jason and Donovan shifted into wolves at that moment, effectively cutting off her tirade, and then moments later they shifted back into men. It hit her that they did so because shifting sped up the healing process exponentially. Both men looked much better, and by their movements, as they continued to smile at her cheekily while getting dressed again, she deduced that they felt better as well. Donovan seemed to move a little slower than Jason, however, given that he got the brunt of Gabe's beating. She assumed it was most likely because he was the Beta after all. He was supposed to be setting the example for the rest of the pack, not ignoring the rules

Donovan pulled April up into a standing position and hugged her close before pulling off the scraps that were once her clothing. When he was done, she trailed her hands down his chest and then over to his ribcage, feeling that they were still severely bruised. She closed her eyes and let the blue sparks filter out of her palms and permeate his body.

"Thank you, my angel." Donovan hugged her close again, fully healed this time. "But the first thing you need to realize is that Gabe is your Alpha now as well. The pack hierarchy exists for a very good reason, and so does its discipline. You'll come to understand in time."

She felt Jason step up behind her and immediately turned in his arms. He was pretty much healed already, but as she snuggled in close to him, she felt something off in his right leg. Again, she let her healing power out, and within seconds, Jason righted his footing. He then sweetly kissed her on the lips while Donovan kissed her neck.

Donovan gave her one more quick squeeze before saying, "As much as I love having you naked between us, you're right that this is neither the time nor the place.

I'm going to go rustle up something for you to wear."

"Good idea, brother. I'd rather avoid having the urge to rip pack members apart for staring at our girl."

April's mood couldn't help but be lifted at their teasing. She laughed and playfully smacked Jason's arm, then turned to do the same to Donovan. He was quick enough to sidestep her, however. And just as he was about to ascend the stairs, she saw clothing fly down, hitting him square in the face.

"From Corrine," came Gabe's booming voice from atop the stairs.

April donned the light green female tracksuit as quickly as she could, considering both Donovan and Jason *helped*. Their help included zipping and unzipping her hoodie several times to play with her breasts. When she swatted them away for the last time, a familiar scent hit her nostrils.

"What is it, love?"

"Nothing." April pushcd passcd Donovan and Jason and headed up the stairs, both her mates in tow. She turned to look at them when she reached the top of the stairs. "Does this smell like anyone you know?" she indicated at the material of the hoodie.

Jason and Donovan both sniffed the material. "Smells like Corrine," Donovan replied. Jason nodded in agreement.

"Hmmm." April turned and proceeded into the den where she heard Gabe and Corrine whispering heatedly.

"A strong healer, indeed," Corrine remarked when they entered the den, looking from Donovan to Jason, neither of whom had a scratch on them. "Am I to also assume that you no longer have the wounds that that pig, Kheelan, inflicted, Jason?"

"Yes, ma'am. Your assumption would be correct."

Turning to Gabe, he added, "Are we cool now, Alpha?"

"As long as there is no further insubordination, we're fine, though I must admit that I very much enjoyed the sparring session."

April let loose another growl and felt her wolf coming close to the surface, but both Jason and Donovan placed their hand on each of her arms and spoke soothingly in her ear. Meanwhile, their arrogant son of a bitch Alpha simply stood there smirking at the three of them. April felt very grateful for the contact at that moment and not just because they were her mates, but because they helped calm her wolf down. She still had very little control over her newfound wolf and feared her taking over any time someone dared pissed her off.

Would serve them right, her wolf chimed in.

Pipe down!

Everyone in the room turned to look at her, and suddenly they all erupted in laughter. Apparently she had chastised her inner wolf out loud. She stomped over to sit on the couch, grumbling underneath her breath until the laughter in the room subsided.

"Your punishment was just, Gabe," Donovan stated, joining her on the couch. Jason sat on the other side of her. "But with all due respect, I can't say that I would have done anything differently, even though I know perhaps I should have."

"That's what makes you a great second, Donovan. Your actions are always well thought out and done for a good reason." April both saw and heard the respect emanating from Gabe for her mate. Perhaps he wasn't as big of an asshole as she thought. "Your mates," he directed at April, "are two of the finest men I know. I know that if they circumvented the rules, right or wrong, they had a damn good reason to do so, especially given the fact that they don't do it often. I would trust them with my life and am proud to have them in my pack." He walked over to sit on the couch across from her, Corrine following and taking a seat beside Gabe. "I recognize not only great strength in you, April, but fierce loyalty and goodness as well. The fates have chosen well for Donovan and Jason, and as Alpha, I am honored to welcome you into our pack."

April felt her eyes welling with tears from Gabe's speech. "Thank you." She knew that her adoptive wolf family back in Washington had loved and accepted her, and by extension, so did their small pack, but she never felt like they were home to her. For the first time in her life, with her mates beside her, she felt like this was where she truly belonged. "I … um … sorry that I growled at you and you know … wanted to … well never mind that part." No need to inform the very powerful Alpha that she wanted to tear him from limb to limb for hurting her mates.

Gabe threw his head back and laughed. "Don't be sorry, April. It's quite natural. Besides, I'm sure it won't be the last time," he added with a wink.

Just then, she heard the front door open, and they all stood when three new arrivals walked in—two wolves and one…

"April," her former dungeon-mate, whose name she learned from her mates was Erica, shrieked right before she launched herself at April. "I'm so glad you're safe," she said when she was done squeezing her. "We were all so worried."

Erica pulled her over to introduce her to Ben and Leo, her mates. After introductions were made, Gabe had apparently had enough with pleasantries.

"Right, let's get down to business. We still have a sadistic fucker to kill and a few things to learn from our

April here."

All eyes were on April now, prompting her to go over the accounts of her captivity from everything she saw within the walls of that other realm to how Frederych tried to pull her powers from her. She decided to skip the conversation she had with Kheelan for now, not wanting to relive that part again just yet. She simply told them that she discovered that her father had been half wolf and that she only learned of her ability to shift a few hours ago. She also left out the part that her discovery was made after being fully mated to Donovan and Jason. They could sort that out for themselves if they wanted to or not.

Corrine remained stoic throughout, but April could tell that she was assessing every detail. Erica and her two mates seemed just as shocked as Corinne and Gabe had been when they discovered that she was also a wolf shifter.

Erica turned to Donovan and Jason. "How did you find her?"

"I had a vision," Donovan replied, "when you touched my arm. It activated something within my tattoo that led us to April. Jason and I had to make sure it wasn't some sort of trick used by Kheelan to lure us into a trap before anyone else got involved."

Corrine strode over to Donovan. "Let me see it," she demanded with urgency. Her eyes widened in shock when Donovan rolled up his sleeve and showed her the intricate design.

April had admired it earlier, but could not make out the symbols. Donovan explained to Corrine about his dream and how he came to have the tattoo on his arm.

"My sister used to draw this design all the time. It started when we were kids. Ilyra told me that it would be important someday and that it would save her—"

April gasped. "Ilyra was my mother."

"Impossible. I was told that her child was dead."

Gabe went over to put his arms around Corrine. April watched as several different emotions flitted across the woman's face—shock, sadness, and perhaps even guilt.

April had no choice then but to recount all that Kheelan had told her and hoped that Corrine could shed some light on the dark tale that Kheelan had woven.

"It makes sense now," Corrine said. "That bastard Thornich had been one of Alefric's supporters. I shouldn't have believed him when he told me you were gone. But your father and mother had both been murdered, and there was no trace of you. I had no choice but to believe him." Corrine got out of Gabe's embrace and slowly approached April. She cupped her face in both of her hands. "I would never have stopped searching for you if I had known you lived."

April nodded, tears pooling in her eyes. No wonder the clothes she wore carried a familiar scent. Corrine was her aunt. It also brought back a memory of her mother's similar fragrance. And she couldn't blame Corrine for not searching for someone she thought had also been murdered. The only ones to blame were Kheelan and his supporters. "Is everything Kheelan told me true then?"

Corrine dropped her hands and went over to sit back on the couch, prompting April to sit beside her. "I knew your father was seeing someone before he met Ilyra, but I didn't know he had a serious relationship with Kheelan. Ilyra never told me, and she had no reason to share her husband's history with past lovers with me or anybody else. It was between them. I know Kheelan, though, better than I would like. The way in which you described your parents' murder and his unwavering attempts at locating you, sounds like vengeance of a lover scorned." She took April's hand in hers. "Your mother and father loved each other very much, sweetling. And they loved you even more. I was devastated when I lost them, but I can't tell you how happy I am that you were not lost, after all."

"Do you know why I couldn't shift until today?" April asked. She had so many questions, so much to learn about both the races that she was made up of, but she'd start with the most important ones for now. "Or why no one, including me, could tell I was Fae or wolf? I lived with a wolf family and their pack for years. I've even treated countless wolves when they were injured. Not once did anyone recognize me as either Fae or shifter."

Corrine patted April's hand and smiled. "Your mother must have administered a powerful potion, knowing her. She was even more skilled than I am at making them. I think she purposely made it so that it would start to wear off when you met your mates, and as for your inner wolf, well, Donovan and Jason are wolves. Let's just say mates have a way of … bringing dormant genes out," she trailed off suggestively.

"Oh," was all she could say. April felt her cheeks reddening and suddenly found the rug very interesting.

"I guess her wolf wanted to come out and play, too." Erica giggled as she came to sit on the couch on April's other side. "Don't be embarrassed. We're all friends here." She gave April's shoulders a quick squeeze before adding with a wink, "Besides, if I was part shifter, you can bet your freckles my wolf would have burst out of me a long time ago."

April threw her head back and laughed. She was

right for thinking that she and this woman would become friends back when they were held captive in the dungeons. Once again Erica had managed to put April at ease. What did she care anyway if they or anyone else knew that her men were amazing lovers, so amazing in fact that their prowess in the bedroom literally made her turn into a wild animal.

Things took a serious note again when Erica vowed, "I promise you, April, Kheelan will pay for what he has done to not just my family, but yours and that of our people as well. We will bring him to justice, and we will save the humans he kidnapped."

"I understand that one of the humans taken is a friend of yours," Gabe stated.

She nodded. "Dee. She was taken the same night that they took Jason." April shivered at the memory. She looked up at Jason to see him watching her intently. She couldn't wait to be in the comfort of his and Donovan's arms again. They barely had any time together, and now they were being thrown right back into chaos. "We barely knew each other, but still, they wanted me and now she's paying the price."

A chorus of "it's not your fault" rang around the room, and though she did know that deep down, it did little to assuage her guilt.

Gabe sat across from April. "Did Kheelan make any mention of the humans at all to you?"

April shook her head. "But as I mentioned, there were a lot of other cells. Soundproofed, I think."

"The place is well hidden. It seems logical that he would be holding them there," Donovan speculated.

"Agreed," Gabe said. "And it's not like he would simply let them go out of the kindness of his heart."

"He's a twisted fuck," Erica added. "He'll find a way for them to be useful to him."

April felt sick thinking about that scenario. As a healer, she was able to survive what had been done to her, but she knew that the humans would most likely not be able to if they didn't get to them soon. She had to also consider the possibility it may be already too late to save them.

Gabe stood. "We'll send in a few men to monitor their comings and goings. If we have a chance to grab someone, we take it." Turning to Donovan, he added with commanding authority, "You will lead this mission."

"Yes, Alpha."

Ben and Leo also volunteered their services. They now ruled the Fae kingdom with Erica, but they also assisted in pack matters as April had just learned. Naturally, Jason, as one of the top enforcers, would be joining them as well as another shifter named Niall, whom April had not yet met.

"I memorized the symbols on my way out," April said. "I'll be able to get us in if we don't see anyone guarding the outside."

"Over my dead fucking body," Jason roared.

The room went silent. She could see in her peripheral vision the others looking back and forth between them.

"Excuse me?" April stood, balling her hands into fists at her side.

"You heard him." Donovan crossed his arms. "We will bring you Kheelan's ashen heart after we rip it out of his chest. Hell, I'll give you a play by play of how much he suffered before he died, but you will never be anywhere near that bastard's vicinity again."

"There will be no ripping out hearts just yet," Gabe said. "This is just a—"

"I wasn't asking for your permission," April

snapped at Donovan then looked pointedly at Jason, and in the process, cut Gabe off, forgetting herself for a moment.

"And yet," Jason waved his hand at her dismissively, "you're still not going."

"But it's okay for the two of you to put yourselves in harm's way while I … what?" She threw her hands up in frustration. "Sit around and wait for the two of you like a good obedient little woman?" she added. "Maybe I'll take up knitting to pass the time." Sarcasm dripped from her tone. "You two have no idea how helpless and worthless I felt while just waiting around at home, and then in the dungeons, and now you want me to do that again? To wonder if you two will come back safely while I do absolutely nothing? Hell, no!"

With that, she stormed out of the den and out of the front door, slamming it shut behind her.

Chapter Fifteen

"Umm, I may have dealt poorly with that," Jason muttered as they all watched April storm across the yard towards the cabin.

"Yeah, no shit, Sherlock." Erica rolled her eyes, and then they narrowed in suspicion as they locked onto Ben and Leo. "And do you think *I'm* going to stay at home while you go hunting for that bastard as well?"

Jason knew a trap when he heard one. He said a silent prayer to the Goddess for his friends to get out of this with their balls still attached and then he pulled Donovan aside.

"I'll go try to smooth this over with April while you get this plan in motion."

"Okay, just try not to fuck it up any more than we already have, brother." Donovan's stress showed as he ran his hands through his hair. "I don't want April to feel like we're not including her, but the thought of her being anywhere near that cave again makes my wolf go insane."

"Mine too," Jason agreed. "I'll do my best to make her see that we just needed to protect her."

Jason must have gone over the conversation he wanted to have with April in his mind about twenty times as he crossed the lawn towards their cabin. He needed to do this without putting his foot in his mouth again.

He entered the cabin expecting to go on the offensive right away, but when he didn't see April, he followed her scent into the master bedroom right up to the closed—and what he assumed was a locked—bathroom door.

His assumption had been correct he realized when he turned the knob.

"April?" Jason put his forehead against the door and concentrated on listening for any sign of her distress. Fortunately, he didn't hear anything out of the ordinary. "Can I come in and talk?" he pleaded.

No answer. Then he heard the sound of water running from the bathtub faucet.

Most shifter females Jason knew would've just rolled their eyes at the dominating outburst he'd had back in Gabe's office. They would have pretended to defer to their mates' need to protect them, and then figured out a way to get what they wanted eventually. Female shifters were diabolical that way. April, however, was fierce in her own need to protect them, just as they sought to protect her. It only made her more attractive to him, and it was all he could do to stop himself from barging in the bathroom, knowing that she was alone and upset … and naked … and wet.

"April, baby?" he tried again.

"Go away, Mr. Wolf bossy-pants." she yelled back.

"April, I'm sorry," he started off apologetically until his temper rose up and he forgot that he was supposed to be groveling. "No, I'm *not* sorry that Donovan and I need to keep safe. And I am not sorry that we don't want you in any more danger. This is what we were put on this Earth *for,* April, to love and protect you, so let me in there so I can see that you're okay."

She didn't answer for a few moments, and then Jason heard the slosh of water as she got out of the tub.

Thank the Goddess, she's listening to me. I'm way better at this mate thing than I thought. I can't wait to rub it in Donovan's face once he gets home!

"Let you in, hmm?" April said in a snarky tone as she wrenched the door open. "Is this what you think our life will be like, Jason? You two ordering me around and me jumping to attention?"

Jason found it difficult to concentrate on a single word that came out of his mate's mouth. Who could expect him to even remember how to breathe when she was standing there, hot from the bath, completely nude? Every glorious freckle just tempting him to fall at her feet and pay homage. She was the most exquisite thing he'd ever seen. The Goddess couldn't have created a more beautiful creature than the woman standing in front of him.

"Well sheesh, Jason." April blushed a deep red, and then a small smile curved at her lips. "It's kinda hard to keep a grudge going when you say stuff like that, but seriously, I can't just stay on the sidelines where you and Donovan want to keep me. That's not who I am, Jason."

Oh shit! Had he said that out loud? *Meh.* Jason didn't so much care if she thought he was cheesy as long as a door no longer separated him from her naked body. He sighed loudly in defeat. He needed to stop looking at his perfect mate for a second if he was going to hope to get his brain working again.

"April, we know who you are, baby," he began, "and it's not that we want to keep you on the sidelines at all, but you only just shifted for the first time today, and it's going to take some time to learn to control the urge to let your wolf out when you get emotional. It will be dangerous if you can't control her in a combat situation. You have to trust us on that. And yes, the thought of Kheelan getting anywhere near you again terrifies me. I felt like my heart was bleeding hearing about what he had done to you."

He watched her think about the implications of his words and hoped she could understand why he and Donovan reacted the way they did. "But I acted like a complete ass at Gabe's, and I'm sorry for that," he added in hopes that his mate might have pity on his addled brain. "I can't think straight when I imagine you in danger. Can you forgive me, baby?"

He knew he had her when the corner of her mouth turned up in a small grin and she opened up the door all the way to invite him in.

"Maybe, but you'll have to make it up to me." April's voice turned husky when she said, "Why don't you strip down and see what you can do about that while I relax in the bath?"

Jason's wolf almost whimpered embarrassingly and out loud at her suggestion, but when she turned around and slowly walked to the steaming bathtub, an exaggerated sway to her heart-shaped ass, he suddenly couldn't care less if his wolf howled his way behind their mate. When she bent to lower herself into the water, he did groan, and he began to undress in record time to join her.

The sound of her giggling laughter was worth getting caught in his pant leg and hopping around like an idiot, and he knew right then that he'd spend the rest of his life doing anything to keep his woman happy.

"Careful there. Don't bruise the merchandise." April winked at him as she leaned back in the water. "Now let me see what I paid for."

Jason loved this playful side of her. This was the woman he had met that first night at the bar, only she seemed stronger now like there was just *more* to her somehow. Her carefree teasing made him forget about everything they'd been through until now, and she made him feel like everything would turn out right.

Once he finally untangled himself from his jeans, he walked towards the tub, trying to ignore the giant erection that was currently pointed straight at his mate.

The quirk of her lips, a slow peek of her tongue, and her raised eyebrow when she took a good long look and finally met his eyes, only made him want her more.

"Behave," he growled playfully as he lowered himself into the water and offered her his hand to join him on the other side of the tub. "It's hard to act all smooth and suave with a naked goddess in the tub with me, you know."

Once again, she giggled as she turned and presented him with the most perfect ass he'd ever seen. She then threw a knowing look over her shoulder and gave him a sexy smile.

"Oh, I can see that," she teased. "I'd say it looks pretty hard."

"Vixen, come here." Jason grabbed her and pulled her down so that she lay between his legs, her smooth back resting against his chest.

They both simultaneously let out a sigh and relaxed into each other, letting the calm wash over them. April absently trailed her fingers up and down his arms while he did the same to her thighs.

She finally broke the silence when she asked, "Did everyone think I was a drama queen for storming out like that?" He felt her cringe in his arms.

"No, love. As a matter of fact, Erica was chewing out her own mates for the exact same reason when I made my escape," he reassured her.

The feel of her fingers caressing him was beginning to interrupt his thought process, causing him to moan. "Goddess, that feels good, April. It's like I can feel your touch all over my body."

Jason closed his eyes as the sensations grew stronger. If he didn't know better, he'd think there was more than one person touching him. He felt her everywhere as if her power became extra phantom limbs. His arousal grew with each stroke of her hands, each phantom touch. He didn't want her to stop anytime soon, but when she slowly turned in his lap and straddled his hips, all he could think about was moving his hips a fraction of an inch and sliding inside of this amazing woman. Through the link that connected all three of them, he could feel a vague irritation coming from Donovan.

Oops. He needed to remember that his brother was currently in a meeting with the rest of the enforcers, attempting to plan the attack on Kheelan. Jason could understand that he wouldn't want to do it with a raging hard-on and that this bond was too new to all of them. They hadn't had time yet to learn to close it off when they needed some privacy.

"April…" He tried to protest—well, he half-assed tried to protest as her soft hands ran all over his body—but come *on* … what did his brother want from him?

"Shh, I know. I just need to touch you," she answered against his lips, her voice low and so sexy it drove him crazy. "This power inside of me feels like a living thing, and when I'm this close to you or Donovan it wants to reach out and caress you like it feels this connection as strongly as I do."

Jason was just about to ask what exactly she meant by that when she placed her palms in the middle of his chest and a bright blue light lit up between them. Suddenly, it felt like someone had just detonated an explosion of the most intense pleasure he'd ever felt inside him. Before he could stop himself, his hips were moving, his shaft sliding in between her pussy lips, and then he yelled out her name as an orgasm was nearly ripped from his body. At the same time, he heard April's moan of pleasure and he knew that she had come as well.

Just as suddenly as it appeared, the light was gone, and April collapsed against him.

"Holy hell! What was that?" he asked once his breath returned to him. He slowly stroked his hands up and down her back. "Are you okay, baby?"

"Yeah, I'm okay." She pulled back and smiled sleepily at him, running her fingers along his skin. "Hmm, I guess my touch can do more than just heal. I wonder what else I can do with it?"

"How did you do that?" Jason laughed at the satisfied look on her face, but his laughter quickly died down when he realized there was one-third of their bond who wasn't feeling all that happy at the moment. "Oh, damn."

"What's wrong?" April asked. She must have felt that Jason had tensed underneath her.

Jason was spared from explaining the reason to April when the bathroom door swung open and in burst Donovan with an extremely unhappy look on his face.

"Do you two want to tell me what the hell is going on in here? You literally made me come in my jeans while I was in a room full of people."

Both Jason and April glanced down at the now dark spot at the front of Donovan's jeans. Then they looked at each other and burst out laughing.

Chapter Sixteen

Donovan could not remember ever being this frustrated, angry, and horny at the same time. He had been sitting in Gabe's office, doing his level best to pay attention to his Alpha, when suddenly it began to feel like his mate was leaning back against him, skin on skin. It had been the most sensual and weirdest feeling of his life. He had known that April was nowhere near him, but by the Goddess, in that moment, he actually smelled the citrus scent of her goddamned shampoo.

"For fuck's sake," Donovan snarled as he glared down at his mate and his brother, both of whom were still laughing like fucking hyenas at his expense. "I sent you a warning with the hope that you would cut a guy some slack and give me a freakin' break so I could get through that damn meeting. But did you? No, you both decided it would be much better to amplify whatever the fuck you had going on in here, and had me coming like an untried teenager in my jeans … in a room full of fucking wolf shifters who knew exactly what had happened and could scent the proof!"

April winced. "I'm so sorry, baby. I don't know how that happened. I wasn't aware that it was affecting you like it was Jason and me."

"I'm not sorry," Jason, the smug bastard boasted as he lay back in the bath water. "That was the most explosive orgasm of my life, and I am not about to regret one single moment of it."

Donovan growled low in his chest as he stomped over to the shower, turning the water on before pulling his shirt over his head. "That's just perfect. I am never going to live that down. Ever." Donovan continued to mutter and complain as he stripped off his jeans, and underwear, grimacing as he drew off the wet material before stepping into the shower. He washed up quickly then put his arm up to rest against the wall under the heavy stream of water, letting the heat relax some of the tension from his shoulders.

In an effort to forget about the single most embarrassing moment of his adult life, he instead thought about what Gabe had been discussing before his dick had taken over. Their Alpha's plan was to go on a little recon mission, and that meant silent in and silent out. Any information they found would help in the fight, and Gabe was giving him the mission lead. It was an honor, and Donovan was determined to do a good job. Especially as the meeting ended with him biting back a roar as his body betrayed his will and him shooting his load in his boxers!

Turning the water off with a sigh, Donovan left the shower and reached for a towel. He glanced over at the bath and saw his brother was still lounging in the water with a look of abject satisfaction on his ugly mug.

Damn. What the hell happened here?

"Brother, you are in for a treat," Jason murmured as he cracked his eyes open and looked over at him. "And if what happened to you is a by-product of what our mate is about to introduce you to, then I am going to enjoy the hell out of it."

Donovan frowned at Jason's cryptic words before dropping his towel in the laundry basket and striding out of the bathroom. His intention was to get dressed and talk to April rationally about why her not being on the mission was really for the best. However, all thought of rational conversation flew out the window at the sight that greeted him in the bedroom.

April knelt on the bed, completely naked, her left hand gently cupping her left breast and her right hand sliding against her wet pussy. Donovan believed his jaw would have dropped directly to the floor, not passing Go, and not collecting two hundred dollars if his tongue had not been stuck to the roof of his suddenly dry mouth.

"Hmmm, I thought you were going to take too long in that shower," April purred as her hands kept moving, holding Donovan mesmerized. "Now, I want to ask you a couple of questions. Will that be okay, Donovan? Just a couple of innocent questions?"

Donovan nodded, still unable to form words. He stumbled toward the bed, his cock now painfully hard and bobbing against his stomach as he walked.

"Lie down on your back beside me, baby," April said in a voice filled with heat and suggestion, and Donovan was helpless to resist. He crawled up on the bed, then rolled to his back beside his mate, his face close to her pussy. He inhaled deeply drawing the scent of his mate's arousal into his lungs, growling at the enticingly spicy fragrance.

He ran his fingers through her wet folds, but before he could touch her, he felt a phantom hand slide along his wrist halting his movement. Startled, he stopped moving and looked up at his mate.

April reached out with the hand that had been delving into her pussy and swept a wet finger across his bottom lip. With a moan, he licked the juicy treat off with his tongue and drew her flavor into his mouth.

"It's okay, Donovan. I just know that if I let you touch me, this will be over before I get to ask my questions, and I *really* want to ask those questions. Put your arms out to the side and spread your legs a little. Let me look at what's mine while we play my little game."

Donovan grinned and moved to comply. "I am loving this side of you, angel. It's hot and sexy as hell."

April smiled wickedly at him as her hand went

back to its slow travels over her pussy. "I'm glad you think so because I think I'm going to love when you give me control in the bedroom. It's not something I will demand every time, but right now, it is a pretty heady feeling. Now, let's get the questions out of the way because I have a need to ride my mate hard."

Donovan's cock twitched at the thought of that.

"Question number one, do you like the fact that I am both Fae and shifter?"

"Hell yes." Donovan's answer was immediate, no hesitation. "Not only is my mate the hottest woman on the planet who can get me rock hard with a single look, but she's someone who can run with me in that form, something I am looking forward to doing soon, and you're a fucking Fae healer? Win, win, win as far as I'm concerned."

April blushed prettily as she moved her hands to his chest, her hands warm against his skin, and gave him a dazzling smile. "That's the perfect answer. You deserve a reward."

Donovan had a split second to wonder what that reward might be before his body lit up with pleasure and he arched up off the mattress. Her palms emitted a blue light against his chest. "Holy mother of fuck!" he roared as what felt like April's hands massaged, and caressed every inch of his skin, and he had no idea how she was doing it, but he could have sworn he felt her mouth wrapped tight around his cock in that moment, too.

Then it stopped, and he collapsed back against the bed, breathing heavily. He heard his brother groan from the bathroom and realized that Jason was feeling a similar pleasurable feedback down their mating link to what he had felt earlier in the meeting.

"What the hell was that?" Donovan's voice was

hoarse.

"Turns out, I can do a lot more with my powers than just heal." April grinned, and her hands on his chest were still glowing with a blue energy. "And it feels just as pleasurable to me as it does to you. Trust me. Now, for question number two. Do you still think I should stay behind when you go on this little recon trip?"

Donovan knew it was a trap. Hell, he could basically hear the sirens going off in his head, but he couldn't lie to his mate. Not now, not ever. "Yes, baby, I do." April's eyes narrowed, and all the pleasure leeched out of his body. He looked down as his cock deflated right before his eyes. "Fuck."

"Nope! There will be no fucking here with an attitude like that," April said rather matter-of-factly as she sat back, and the heat and pleasure that had been burning in her eyes moments before had banked down to a simmer. "As I explained to your brother, I am a partner in this relationship, and I am not the type of woman who can sit back and keep the home fires burning while the menfolk go off to war. I need you to respect that, and I have proven that I could handle myself. How can I be worthy of the two of you otherwise?"

Donovan's eyes narrowed. She had a lot to learn, not just about being a wolf, but about her own self-worth, and about being mated. He moved to sit up, but found that his limbs were locked in position. "April, let me up."

"No." Her bottom lip came out, and she pouted prettily at him. "I am not letting you up until you come to your senses."

Donovan growled, and his wolf began to pace agitatedly within him. "Then we might be here for a fucking long time. You ask me to see your side and respect it, but you are not willing to do the same. You are our *mate,* April. Worthy of us as we will strive to be worthy of *you*, and let me fill you in how this mating thing works while I'm at it. You are everything to Jason and me. There is no Donovan without you. There is no Jason without you. If anything happened to you, it would kill us both. If you were hurt when we could have prevented it, or Gods forbid, taken from us, then we would follow. We would have no choice. And this is not about the goddamn bond or some magical connection that exists because of our mating claim. This is about the fact that I gave you my heart and Jason gave you his, and we are doing everything in our power to convince you to give us yours in return.

"But I also know that you are strong. Hell, baby, you got yourself out of that lab without our help. You fought that bastard with everything within you, and you were willing to go a round or five with our Alpha for us. So as much as it kills me to say no to you, I don't want you on this mission. You just shifted for the first time, and there is still a lot about being a wolf that you need to learn before you rush into any situation. I would say the exact same thing to any member of our pack, male or female. I do want you standing and fighting right beside me, to help us to rid the earth realm, the Fae realm, hell every damn realm that exists, of that fucker Kheelan, but I am making this decision as Beta of our pack, not just as your mate. Instead of asking us to come to our senses, maybe you can try to see it from our points of view.

"Now, the scent of your arousal is driving me crazy, and despite the fact that you stole my erection, I want you to fuck me into the goddamn mattress, so get on with your questions and take me into your sweet body, or release me from these bindings and leave me to my misery."

A breathless silence met his emotional speech,

and Donovan watched his woman, waiting to see what she did next. Horror filled him when he saw moisture gathering in her eyes, and he was about to apologize for everything but saw the sweetest smile grace her beautiful face.

"I have already given you my heart. You both had it from the very first day—Jason at the diner, and you, when I heard your voice on the phone," she whispered moments before a heat began to build in his chest below her hands. "I realize we aren't always going to agree on everything, so let's just agree to disagree for now."

Donovan relaxed back into the magical hold she had on him and watched as she lifted herself up and swung her left leg over his hips so that she straddled him. *I have already given you my heart.* He smiled wide at the words repeating themselves in his head. The heat on his chest lifted slightly when she moved a hand down to press the head of his cock against her pussy, and then in a move he could do nothing but appreciate the hell out of, she rolled her hips in a tight circle and took him to the hilt.

"Fuck! Hot, tight," Donovan growled as his mate began to slide up his cock, then slam back into him, fucking him into the mattress just like he wanted.

"You might … want to… hold on to something," April panted, and he stared up into her beautiful face, her red hair falling in a silken curtain around her, but it was the emotion swirling in her eyes that had him holding his breath. She was stunning.

Then, somehow she was everywhere again, touching him, stroking him, phantomly sucking him deep into the wet hot cavern of her mouth, even as her pussy rippled tightly around him. Donovan cried out at the pleasure that slammed through him, and he arched his back off the bed. He wanted to reach up and wrap his arms around April, but she still held his arms and legs immobile and the sensation was hot and frustrating at the same time.

April arched her back, and light seemed to burst from inside her. Pleasure slammed through him, driving him into the hardest orgasm of his life. His entire body locked for a moment as he heard his brother shouting his release in the bathroom and his mate screaming hers above him. Then his orgasm crashed over him, and he roared her name to the heavens, pledging his life and his love for her in that one single perfect moment.

Chapter Seventeen

It had been exactly five minutes since Donovan, Jason, and their merry band of wolves had left for their recon mission. Five minutes that seemed more like five hours to April. The idea of letting more minutes go by while all she did was wait and made herself sick with worry in the process, seemed unfathomable to her. She hadn't actually uttered the words that she, in fact, *agreed* to stay behind, only that she agreed to disagree. It certainly wasn't her problem if that was the impression her mates got.

She threw open the front door to the cabin, but before she could exit, two sets of hands were pushing her back inside.

"You're going to have to be a lot stealthier than that," Erica pointed out. Corrine hummed her agreement. "Naturally, we're going to use the back door, but first," Erica whipped out a long blade with symbols she was beginning to recognize as belonging to the Fae language, and handed it to her, "I am going to give you a quick lesson on how to swing this bad boy. You've already got the super juice necessary to do some major damage I presume, given how you blasted your way out of that secret mad science lab and all. Pretty badass, I must say."

"She *is* my niece," Corrine added with a proud smile and a wink at April. "I'd expect nothing less."

April returned her smile, already feeling a bond forming with her newly discovered aunt. She felt a similar bond forming with Erica as well, recognizing a kindred spirit in her. "How did the two of you know I'd follow after them?"

Erica and Corrine exchanged glances before they burst out laughing. "I knew your intent as well as mine and Erica's the minute you stormed out of the den,"

Corrine stated, "and it wasn't because of my Seer abilities."

"Besides, the last time that I left on a mission on my own, Ben and Leo came for me, so now it's my turn to follow them," Erica explained. "And sometimes our men need saving, too. I mean how did those idiots think they were going to get inside should they need to without someone of the Fae persuasion to open the portal through the Veil for them?"

"Idiots, indeed." Corrine harrumphed.

"Speaking of *our* men," Erica turned to Corrine, "where does Gabe think you are?"

"Don't start that with me again, Erica. He's not *mine*. I told you it was far more complicated that you can imagine."

"But he loves you. Anyone with eyes and half a brain can see that."

Corrine gave Erica a look that silenced her immediately. Erica may be the Queen, but it was obvious that Corrine was no one to be messed with. April had noticed earlier how she and Gabe continuously snuck looks at one another when they thought no one would notice, and how Corrine seemed to be the only one who could sway Gabe after he'd made up his mind on a subject. She'd just assumed they were an item.

"I told Gabe I was tired, going to nap in my room and did not wish to be disturbed. Now then," Corrine waved a hand dismissively, "are we going to stand around here all day, or are you going to show our April here some moves so we can get the hell out of here?"

The latter option won. April knew, after Erica expertly demonstrated different ways to swing the blade, that it would take her years to master the art, but as she held the blade in her hands, it almost felt like an extension of her. She didn't need to have mastery in it yet to exude her power with it. She sliced the air from left to right and then back, hearing a whooshing sound with each pass, and then she felt the vibrations coursing through her body as the entire blade glowed from her blue spark.

"Oh yeah! I can do some serious damage with this baby."

Corrine smiled sadly at her. "That blade belonged to your mother." She explained that she had kept it safely with her ever since Ilyra's death, but had never used it as if she'd known that it was not meant for her. April couldn't help the choked up feeling she got as she looked at the blade anew.

After practicing for a few more minutes, she felt confident that she wouldn't be a menace with the blade. She didn't have the years of experience with a sword that Erica and Corrine did, so it would have to be her powers that would prove her worth in the coming battle, but the fact that her weapon had belonged to her mother made it seem as if Ilyra would be with her, protecting her once again. Corrine and Erica both brandished their own curved blades with similar markings. She could tell that both women would be nothing short of fierce in combat.

With another lesson in stealth, the three of them managed to leave the grounds undetected. She was very much impressed, especially when they came across a green jeep parked less than a mile away and Erica prompted them all to get in.

"I have my ways," she winked as she started up the ignition. "I am Queen after all."

Fortunately, April had memorized the way back to the cliff on the drive home with Donovan and Jason and then after parking the jeep out of sight, she led them the rest of the way on foot.

"This is as far as we go for now," Erica whispered. "Otherwise, the guys will pick up our scent and get distracted."

They crouched low behind the cover of tall grass and surrounding bushes not too far from the river that April had rested beside after first escaping. The proximity of the river would also help in the masking of their scent. Now that April knew how to focus her enhanced vision, she could see the cave entrance in the far off distance, even now as darkness fell upon them. The men, however, were out of sight.

Their plan was to do their own recon at first and assist should the wolves encounter any problems or realize that they needed to gain access beyond the Veil to get through the entrance of the cave. Secretly, April hoped to witness their "duh" moment. Jason and Donovan may have been right about the fact that her lack of control over her wolf would be her weakness, but their overpowering need to protect her was theirs.

She'd already mentally prepared herself for a fight just in case, despite learning that Fae would turn to ash if killed outside of the Veil. A cold shiver ran up her spine at the thought of seeing that, and yet, it completely subsided when she pictured Kheelan as nothing more than a pile of dust. That must have been what Donovan had meant when he told her he'd bring back his ashen heart. A wicked smile had formed on her lips at the thought of that, her wolf approving of the idea, but it was quickly replaced by a frown.

"Is that what would happen to the three of us?" she suddenly asked Corrine and Erica, recalling their earlier conversation in the car.

"What?" Corrine and Erica both asked in unison.

"If *we* die in this realm, do we become nothing

more than ash?"

Erica bit her lip and remained silent, but Corrine, after a pensive moment, answered her. "You and Erica will not. You both are mated to wolves and therefore, your spirits have strong ties to both realms, although, April, since you are part wolf, you've always had ties to both."

"What difference does it make?" Erica muttered quietly, looking straight ahead. "Dead is dead. Doesn't matter if we have a body to bury or ashes to scatter."

April wished she'd never asked. The idea that there was even a remote chance of seeing Corrine as nothing but ash was horrifying to her as well. She let the subject drop and turned to focus her attention where it should be at the moment.

"Those three stones above the crevice are definitely not a product of natural formation. They were put there," Corrine remarked.

They looked almost like giant headstones and upon closer inspection, she saw ancient Fae symbols on them. "Holy crap!" The symbols changed right before her eyes. "Did you guys see that?"

Corrine gasped. "Impossible."

"What does it mean?" Erica asked, concern lacing her tone.

April found herself concerned as well. Corrine's ominous expression implied that the stones could only be nefarious. She watched Corrine's lips moving as she silently read the changing symbols.

"If those are the same symbols I think they are, they should have been lost to the Fae hundreds of years ago," she turned to look at April, "along with the people who created them. Tell me more about this Frederych. What powers did he possess?"

"You mean other than making me feel like my

insides were trying to become outsides?"

"Shh!" Erica held up her hand to silence them and looked as if she listened intently.

Then April heard a rustling noise, and within moments, they found themselves face to face with four angry wolf shifters. The fifth one hung back holding onto a very bloodied Fae guard, whom April immediately recognized. She had blasted him out of her way during her escape, after all.

"What the hell do you think you three are doing?" Jason snapped through gritted teeth.

"I suggest you to tone it down, wolf," Corrine snapped back. She stood up from her crouched position, seeming a lot taller than her five-foot-four frame. "Typically speaking, I believe you're the ones meant to heel. Not the other way around."

April would have died laughing from the identical five jaw drops if her men didn't look so angry. Ben and Leo looked none too pleased either as they glared at their own mate, and, Niall, she assumed his name was, looked as if he wanted to laugh after the shock of her statement wore off.

"While you cavemen beat your chests, vowing to protect your women, and storming off to save the day," Corrine continued to the men who wisely chose to remain silent, "not one of you considered the possibility that you might need assistance opening up the entryway. Even the big bad Alpha man himself didn't think to ask to borrow a skilled guard or two from Erica." She tilted her head to the side and looked at Niall and the bloody charge he had hold of. "Apparently, though, you did not need our assistance."

It was Niall who spoke next. "We found this one patrolling the outside. We are taking him back for questioning."

"Gabe and I had already decided against going through the Veil," Donovan said matter-of-factly. "Entering their territory without knowing how many Fae we would run into would not have been prudent." He continued to keep his cool when he added, "We also had Ishaya on standby. There is another Veil entrance not too far from here, and he offered to sneak in and do recon inside if need be."

April suddenly felt bad for doubting them. Obviously, these wolves were not just deadly, but highly trained soldiers. She'd been on her own so long now that learning to rely on others was proving to be more difficult than she'd realized. She knew her mates were strong and dependable, but she couldn't lie to herself either. Her decision to follow would still have been the same, be it a recon mission or a bloody battle because her need to protect them was as strong as theirs was to protect her.

"Well," Corrine looked at April and Erica, both of whom had already stood up. "Our assistance was not needed after all. No harm done. Shall we all go then?" She turned back to the men. "Or should we stick around? We might get lucky and get a chance to see April in action with her new blade fighting skills."

Both Donovan and Jason growled, and April immediately stood in between them and Corrine. No point in goading them any further. She understood all too well a wolf's fierce and sometimes even irrational need to protect its mate, whether the danger was real or imagined.

Suddenly the scent of blood, familiar blood, hit her nostrils. She turned to look at Donovan and Jason and saw that they both sported identical bite marks on opposite arms. "Oh my God. You're both bleeding."

She picked up each of their arms to examine them. Erica and Corrine moved in closer to get a better look, too.

"It's nothing," Donovan said, waving them off. "That fucker bit us." He inclined his head toward the captive Fae.

Erica looked astonished. "Since when do Fae bite?"

"We're fine," Jason dismissed, clearly still miffed, but when he took April's hand in his, he did it gently and not out of anger. "Let's get out of here. We need some answers out of him and a more discreet place to make him a bit more cooperative."

"Okay, but as soon as we get back, I need to look at those wounds. Both of you."

Donovan took her other hand, and they began walking toward the road, the rest of their party following suit. When they had almost reached the jeep—the men had a small van parked nearby—Donovan howled in pain and fell to his knees. Moments later, Jason had the same reaction.

April dropped to her knees as well, placing a hand on each of the bite marks, and watched in horror as her healing power had absolutely no effect on the wound.

"Erica," she cried out. Erica quickly kneeled beside her and placed her hands on top of April's, increasing their healing power tenfold and still nothing happened.

Panic threatened to choke her when she saw blood trickling out of Jason and Donovan's noses and from the corners of their eyes. She saw them both struggling to stifle their grunts of pain, and she knew it was for her sake.

"What's happening? Why can't we heal them?"

she asked no one in particular.

A loud cackling laughter came from the Fae. "It's a gift made especially for you, April ... from Kheelan."

His laughter was cut short when Niall punched him in the face and knocked him out.

"Hurry," Corrine said, "let's get them back to the house. I have my potions there."

But April feared that if her and Erica's combined healing power didn't work, nothing else would work either. She closed her eyes, trying not to let the darkness overtake her at the thought of losing her mates.

Chapter Eighteen

April held her mates' hands in the back of the truck as she tried to send them reassuring thoughts through a link that was becoming narrower with each painful gasp of breath that they took. She tried to shield them from the rage that was quickly spiraling out of her control when she thought about what Kheelan had done to Jason and Donovan. Whatever that bastard had infected them with was moving quickly through their system. The angry looking bite marks now had ash gray skin all around them.

When the truck finally skidded to a stop in the driveway in front of Gabe's house, the rest of their group quickly helped her and her mates out of the back seat. Her men were barely conscious now, and when Niall dragged the bloodied guard out of the second vehicle, a smug look crossed the Fae's face along with a low chuckle.

"Looks like they're almost out of time," he said looking directly at April.

And that was all it took.

She didn't even realize that she had leaped towards him screaming, separating him from Niall's clutches. Her nails searched out the parts of his body that would inflict the most damage. She wanted to take *everything* from him—his hatred, his fear, his blood, his very *soul*. She wanted to leave nothing of him behind, and she felt like she could actually do it.

Everything around April took on an eerie gray tint, and she heard Erica's loud gasp from somewhere behind her.

"April, no!" Erica yelled as she grasped April's arms. "You cannot use your powers like that!"

"He deserves to die, Erica," she wailed as she tried to reach for him once again. "He's killing my mates, and I won't let him!"

"Everyone inside," Erica ordered the rest of the group as she held April in a vise-like grip. "I've got this. Corrine, do what you can for them. I need to speak with April alone."

"What?" April snapped at Erica when she finally released her. "I need to be with Jason and Donovan."

Erica just stood there looking at her. Her distraught expression made April cringe at the tone she'd used.

Finally, Erica spoke. "You're very powerful, April. You found by instinct what took me a long time to figure out about my own abilities, but you must respect that these gifts are given to us by the Goddess herself and they are not to be used lightly or abused. I know you are terrified for your mates, and we will do everything in our power to save them, but you had begun to draw the life force from that Fae just now, and that isn't something I can let you do."

"I heard that that's how you and your mates were able to defeat the King, and I felt your powers shaking the entire castle when I was in the dungeons. Seems a bit hypocritical saying that you won't let me use my powers like that, doesn't it?" April finished her last sentence through gritted teeth and regretted the words as soon as they came out of her mouth, especially when she saw the look of hurt on Erica's face.

"Oh, I'm sure you *could* very easily kill that guard, April," Erica began, "but what I'm trying to tell you is that misusing your gifts *always* comes with a price. Using your powers to harm another should only be used as a last resort, and only in self-defense. The ability to draw another's life-force comes from your healing energy and that comes at an even bigger cost, possibly even your own life. I may have survived, but don't think for a moment that I haven't paid for using mine to end Alefric's reign of terror, because I have. I've paid more than I ever imagined I could."

The strain in Erica's voice while uttering the last sentence was painful to hear. April was afraid to ask her what had happened, but when Corrine stepped out of the back door and placed her hand on Erica's arm, her friend broke down in a tortured sob.

****

"Tell us, Eyrica," Corrine held her, letting her cry. "She came to you? What was the price our Goddess demanded of you, child?"

Erica took a moment to wipe the wetness from her face, and then she stared off into the open sky as she recalled every second of her vision from the Goddess.

"She came to speak to me in a dream the night after we had won the battle. She was more glorious than I ever could have imagined, Corrine," she said with a sad smile. "Has she ever come to you?"

Corrine smiled and nodded.

"The feeling of utter peace and love I felt while in her presence, April, I can't even begin to do it justice. It's inexplicable. She surrounded me like a warm blanket on a cold day. Her voice sounded like a soothing summer stream, though the words she had said to me were anything but soothing."

Erica took a deep breath before she continued to tell them the rest of her dream, a dream that crushed her soul in the end.

"My child, I needed to bring you this news face to face. I couldn't be more proud of how you stood up to Alefric, to end his terror of my people, but you had to

know that the healing gift I have blessed you with was never intended to be used for harm. And when you open your soul up to the darkness like that, there is always a cost."

"I know, my Goddess, but as the True Queen to my people, it was my duty to bear the burden of punishment." Erica lowered her gaze in respect to her Goddess.

"And bear it you will," the Goddess said with sadness. "Your soul was corrupted when you nearly drained Aelfric dry of his life force. I am afraid this means you will never know the gift of creating a life yourself, my daughter."

Erica told Corrine and April of the shock and pain that had rolled through her when she awoke. She had felt as if her heart would shatter into a million pieces. Tears had streamed down her face and her body shook as Leo and Ben had tried to get her to share what had upset her, but it had taken her weeks to find the courage to finally tell them what the price had been for defeating their enemy. She felt the guilt of not being able to give them the family she knew they'd been dreaming of, weighing heavily on her chest. Of course, her mates did not fault her for it, though they had all lost a future barely yet imagined, a powerful bloodline that would have been important to both Fae and shifter kind alike.

Erica would never feel the miracle of a life being created inside of her, furthering the proof of their undying love for each other. No joyful trilling of a child's laughter dancing through their home. No little boys with Leo's serious gaze, or with Ben's playful nature. No daughters that looked just like their mother. She would never hold her babies to her breast, never rock them to sleep in her arms, or see them grow and blossom. This was the price she and her mates would all pay for their service to their people. This was the price of being a Queen.

The looks of pity and sadness on Corrine and April's faces once she had finished her tale, was one of the reasons Erica hadn't told the rest of the pack about what had happened. There had been no need to spread such pain, but now she had no choice. Erica simply couldn't risk the same thing happening to April. There was no way to undo her own sacrifice to stop a tyrant, but she would make damn sure that April didn't pay the same cost especially not out of a blind need for revenge.

"Oh, Goddess. What did I almost do?" April's whisper was almost inaudible as her hand came up to cover her mouth.

"You didn't, April," Erica said. "That's what matters."

"We will find a way to fix what Kheelan has done with his hatred and greed," Corrine promised. "Your mates need you now more than ever, April. Come now, both of you." Corrine took April's hand and led her back into the house, Erica walking beside them. They found the rest of the group gathered around Jason and Donovan in the den.

Erica noticed that a bluish paste now covered the almost identical bite marks on each of their arms and figured that Corrine had administered it to them when she had gone inside when they'd arrived. She could see no visible change in their condition, however.

Chapter Nineteen

A sound of desperation and loss burst from April when she entered the den that was currently turned into a makeshift infirmary. The sight of her mates lying so still on the cots that were lined up side by side in the middle of the room almost dropped her to her knees. Both men had some thick blue paste on their wounds that Corrine had concocted. The blood that had been leaking from their noses and eyes had finally stopped, and the evidence that there had been blood in the first place was cleaned up. April had a feeling, though, that the blue paste was only a Band-Aid, not something that would cure them of whatever poison Kheelan had infused them with through the Fae's bite.

Everyone in the room looked somber, and no one would meet her gaze as Corrine and Erica led her forward. April swallowed the scream she felt building, refusing to let her emotions erupt again.

"Don't lose faith, April," Corrine whispered. "Both your men are still alive. I sense that they are fighting to stay with you, but they are going to need your help to do it."

April took a deep breath, desperately trying to calm the hysteria that was rapidly building inside of her. "What do I do?"

Erica guided her to stand in the small gap between the beds. "Try healing them again. I will help if I can, but I have a feeling that this one is going to fall solely on you."

April stared into Erica's eyes and nodded. Her heart still bled for the woman who had lost so much all in the name of protecting the ones she loved. It all seemed so unfair.

Closing her eyes, April reached a hand out to lay

against each of her mate's chests. She had to fight the urge to draw her hands back when she encountered the cool feel of their skin, completely at odds to the heat that usually radiated from them. Closing her eyes and calling forward her powers, she sent her healing life force out and into the men she was so desperate to save.

When she opened her eyes, she immediately knew that something was wrong. She wasn't looking at their injury or purging them of the poison they had been inflicted with. This was different. She found herself standing alone within a barren landscape, something that reminded her of images she had seen of the desolate frozen tundra far in the north. The light was dim, the air thick with the acrid smell of sulfur that hurt her nose and had her eyes watering almost immediately.

The moment was so unexpected, it startled her and made her lose the connection. She found herself standing back in the den at Gabe's house, staring into the concerned faces of the people around her.

"What the hell was that?" Her voice trembled in shock.

Gabe stepped forward, concern written all over his face. "You know, you took the words right out of my mouth, except mine contained an expletive or seven. You totally zoned out on us there, April. You were physically standing in the room, but mentally you weren't here. Where did you go? You got this strange damn glow about you that had my wolf going crazy. What—"

"Please, Gabe," Corrine interrupted him, and Gabe turned to look at her, his eyes narrowed in displeasure, obviously not happy at being cut off. "Perhaps instead of asking a thousand questions and not letting her speak, you could just let her tell us what happened?"

Corrine turned back toward April, ignoring the now growling Alpha in the room. "I have a feeling you saw something you weren't ready for. Tell us."

April hadn't removed her hand from Donovan and Jason, and it felt as if their skin had cooled even further. "I sent my powers and my consciousness out of myself, in search of the poison to try to purge it from their system, but it felt as if my mind and body were hijacked and transported somewhere. A place that was cold and filled with ice, and so very unforgiving. It was dark, not like it is at night, but more how it is at dusk during a storm, with not a star shining. And the air was thick with the smell of sulfur."

April gasped as Corrine said the last word at the same time. Corrine's face had drained of color, and when she lifted a hand to push her hair from her face, April noticed that it trembled. "The Shadow Realm. How in the hell did he open the Shadow Realm?" Corrine whispered almost as if only to herself.

"Corrine, what is the Shadow Realm?" Gabe asked.

Corrine sighed and moved closer to April to place a hand first on Donovan and then on Jason. As soon as she connected with both men, she gasped and pulled her hands away as if burnt.

"Corrine!" Gabe yelled as he stepped forward and pulled the Fae woman back against his chest.

"I'm okay, Gabe." Corrine calmed the large man by sliding a hand over the arm he had wrapped around her waist. "Somehow, Kheelan has drawn April's mates into the Shadow Realm, a place that exists between this life and the next. It is a place of desolation that can consume the souls that end up there, and if he has locked Donovan and Jason within it, then he has used some very old and very dark magic to drag them into it through that poison he created."

"Okay, but how do I get my mates back from there?" April asked impatiently, not liking the look on the Seer's face.

"I don't know," Corrine said in a tortured whisper. "The people who were able to access that realm have been lost to us for a very long time. I'm not sure if there is anyone who can tell us how to get them back."

April stared at the woman in disbelief. "No, I refuse to accept that. There is some way to get them back because I fucking will not have it any other way. Do you hear me? My mates are hanging on, waiting for the people who care for them most in this world to come and save them. They will not remain in that hideous place. So torture, flay, kill whoever you have to. I don't care. Just find me the answer to saving my mates!"

"April, I think you need to—"

"No!" April yelled, cutting Erica off. She knew she sounded crazy, but she didn't care. "I am not listening to anything else that does not have to do with getting my men back."

"April!" This time, it was Gabe who raised his voice, trying to get her attention. He inclined his head towards Donovan. "I am not sure if this has anything to do with getting your men back, but it is certainly concerning. Does it look like Donovan's tattoo is moving to anyone else?"

****

Donovan dropped to his knees on the ice, his breaths coming way too fast, and his heart felt as if it might burst right from his chest. Running was second nature to wolves and as natural and easy as breathing, but here, where he and Jason had been locked in this fucking hellhole of a place for what felt like an eternity, even walking required some effort. For the briefest of moments, though, he had been certain that he'd felt the presence of his mate. They took off in the direction they had felt her, only for the sensation of her presence to disappear before they could reach her.

"Fuck!" Jason roared from beside him. Donovan turned to look at him, only to find his brother also on his knees, clutching his own chest.

When they had first woken up in this strange and frozen barren landscape, they had searched for any other sign of life but found nothing. They scaled one rocky outcrop to get an idea of where they might be, but there was nothing beyond it but more land and ice as far as their eyes could see. It seemed to go on forever. The place felt altogether surreal, and it made Donovan wonder if this was all a dream or if they had been pulled into some sort of other dimension. He saw no signs of a sun or moon, no stars in the sky that remained a constant dark gray, and the stench that hung thick in the air was becoming increasingly more painful to his highly sensitive nose.

And yet, the longer they stayed, the more *real* it all started to become, as if they now belonged in this place. The air also gradually started to feel colder, and the smell of the sulfur began to increase and burn their noses. Donovan was starting to worry. If they were becoming more corporeal here, wherever the fuck *here* was, what was happening to their bodies back in the real world?

Despite how bleak their situation seemed, it got even worse when they both reached for their wolves, and found them gone.

"What in the hell do we do now?" Jason asked.

Donovan shook his head while looking straight ahead. He rocked back on his haunches, drawing air into his lungs, and fought to remain calm. "I have no idea."

When Donovan looked at Jason again, his jaw dropped at what he saw standing just over Jason's right shoulder. Jason looked at him in confusion before he turned his head to see for himself what got his brother's attention. Had Donovan not been in such a state of shock, he would have laughed as Jason cursed and fell backward onto his ass.

Standing before them, wearing an unearthly-looking white dress embroidered with gold lace, was a beautiful woman with long blonde hair, startling blue eyes, and when she smiled at them, dimples appeared in her cheeks. Whether it was the lighting in this strange world or frostbite seeping into his brain that had his eyes playing tricks on him, Donovan could not tell, but there was an ethereal glow about her that had him thinking perhaps she was an angel come to guide him and Jason to the other side.

He shook his head at the stranger, locking his gaze with hers. "No! Not happening, angel."

Her smile grew wider. "What's not happening, Donovan Olson?" Her voice was just as he suspected it would be, soft, feminine, and celestial.

"We aren't going with you. I don't care if we have to stay in this forsaken barren world of ice for the rest of our lives, we are not going on to the next life without our mate. She lives, we live. Simple as that."

The angel tilted her head to the side, her expression almost quizzical. "Don't you remember me coming to you before, young wolf?"

Donovan frowned for a moment before a memory struck him. "You're the woman in my dream, the one who told me to get my tattoo." Donovan held out his arm, pulling up the sleeve of his shirt to show her he had done as she had asked. "You are Ilyra, April's mother."

Jason cursed, then slammed a hand over his mouth, but the angel nodded with a smile. Tears formed in the woman's blue eyes as she whispered her daughter's name in the Fae tongue. Ilyra took a deep breath, her gaze falling to the tattoo on Donovan's arm.

"I foresaw what would happen to my beloved daughter and her mates, and what would be needed to release you from this realm. Our family had already lost so much because of that monster, and I could not bear Apriell losing anymore. Your tattoo will serve its second purpose to assist you now in escaping this prison."

"How?" Jason asked. "Do you know what this place is?"

"You are in the Shadow Realm. It is unnatural for you to be here, lost in this place that exists between the darkness of the otherworld and the light of yours. You need the tattoo to save yourselves."

Donovan pushed up to stand before the angel, shocked at how weak he felt. "Save ourselves from what? What's coming for us here?" Donovan reached down and helped Jason to his feet.

The angel's eyes turned sad, and Donovan suddenly didn't want to hear what she was going to say. "Save you from death, young wolf. Even now the poison draws you and your brother further into this realm. Eventually, you will cease to exist in your realm, and you will be lost. I cannot let that happen." Ilyra gave them a small smile. "Apriell deserves a chance to live a life of love and happiness, and that will only occur if the two of you are by her side. To give her that life, you must survive this attack, and you must fight for her. Another battle is coming. She and your pack will need your help to win it."

"And we will give it," Jason promised as he

swayed on his feet.

Donovan could feel the poison spreading through his now ice cold veins, Ilyra's words about dragging them further into this realm ringing true. He nodded. "Damn straight we will. Now, tell me how to get this ink on my arm to work its magic. Jason and I are done with this place. We want to get back to our mate."

Ilyra reached toward Donovan's tattoo but paused before she made contact. "Tell my daughter that I will love her forever and one day we will all be reunited. Oh, and give a message to my sister. Tell her that time grows short. Her fate is bound to them, and she must act soon."

Donovan and Jason agreed to pass along the message, though Donovan had no clue what she was talking about in reference to Corrine. Ilyra touched the ink on Donovan's arm, and he felt a stream of fire burn beneath his skin as if the flame had been set to the ink itself. It burned a path all along the tattoo. He heard another voice chanting, one as familiar to him as his own, but he was in too much pain to seek her out. Suddenly, it became difficult for him to draw breath, and his heartbeat quickened, the sound of it thumping, thundering in his ears. The world of ice beneath him shattered. He could have sworn he heard a man in the distance scream with rage, moments before he and Jason were pulled through the shattering ice.

Donovan felt as though they were falling fast through a vortex of ice. The air felt so thick and heavy around him that made it hard to draw any oxygen into his lungs. Just when he felt like he would suffocate, he tried to use his last remaining breaths to utter his mate's name, but instead of saying her name, he drew in April's scent and the smell of fresh air.

With a growl, he sat up, searching for the source

of the sweet scent. He found himself sitting in a bed in the middle of Gabe's den with several confused-looking shifters and Fae women all staring at him and Jason.

"Oh, Goddess, thank you!" April sobbed before she swayed alarmingly.

Donovan reached out, and pulled her up and onto the bed with him, wrapping her in his arms. Jason moved swiftly from where he sat on the bed opposite, to nestle himself against April's other side. The two of them held her tight as she continued to sob.

"It's okay, baby," Jason murmured to their mate. "We're here."

Donovan's body ached, and when he reached for his wolf, he was relieved to feel his beast there, pacing in anger at what had happened to them. "I heard you chanting, April."

"Your tattoo held the incantation that saved you," Corrine replied as she moved to place a hand gently on Donovan's arm. "My sister must have foreseen this, too, and wove the spell into the ink on your arm. In the moment you needed it most, it resettled itself into the words April needed to bring you back from the Shadow Realm."

"We saw Ilyra in the Shadow Realm," Donovan said. April lifted her tearstained face to look at him, her eyes wide with shock. "She helped us get back to you."

Jason pressed a kiss to April's cheek and nuzzled close to her neck. "Your mom wanted us to tell you that she loves you and that one day, you will see her and your father again."

April hiccup-laughed, a sound that Donovan found adorable, and he pressed her even tighter against his chest. Then he remembered the second part of Ilyra's farewell message they were to bring back with them.

Donovan looked at Corrine. "Your sister had a

message for you, too. She wanted us to tell you that time is growing short. Your fate is bound to them, and you must act soon."

"What the hell does that mean?" Gabe all but snarled. "Whose time is running short, and who is the '*them*' that your fate is fucking bound to?"

Donovan winced. The air around them thickened as Gabe's dominance filled the room.

Corrine swallowed visibly and turned to stare at the Alpha. "*My* time is running short, and the '*them*' that she is referring to," Corrine hesitated a moment then stood tall with her head high, "are my mates."

Chapter Twenty

"No!" Kheelan screamed and threw the glass sphere he held in his hand across the room, watching it hit the wall and shatter. That window into the Shadow Realm was useless to him now anyway. "You said they would be trapped in the Shadow Realm, Frederych. You said they would die!"

Frederych seemed unfazed by his outburst as he continued to examine the human corpse on the table in front of them. Finally, he looked up. "You saw them escape? Hmm, that should not have been possible. How curious. The poison I infused into your Fae guard should have left them to die in the realm beyond."

"Then *how* did they escape, you imb—" Kheelan was furious, but he had to remember that making an enemy of Frederych was not in his best interest, so he reined it in. Also, the man did manage to mostly patch him up from that traitorous bitch, Corrinc's fatal stab wound, so he hadn't been completely useless, and not all of the experiments they'd tested on the filthy humans had proven worthless. He no longer had to administer a healing patch daily.

His strength had returned, in fact, and he had never felt better with all the added touches Frederych had performed, but all of it was still only temporary. He had intended to recapture April, drain her of her powers, and transfer them onto himself before he killed her, thus allowing himself the ability to heal. Taking her mates away from her would have just been a bonus, a prelude to the misery he had in mind for her. Clearly, he had overestimated Frederych's abilities and wondered if he could have found someone stronger to assist him. Then suddenly, the possibility that his enemies had found someone stronger hit him. "Do they have one of *your* kind aiding them?"

"Impossible." Frederych scoffed at his accusation.

It irritated Kheelan that the other male had no fear of him. Fear would have been a much better motivator when it came to working under him.

"Oh? Why do you think that is impossible, Frederych, if I managed to find you, after all? Or have *you* perhaps betrayed me?"

Frederych didn't look in the least bit affronted at Kheelan's accusation. If anything, he looked bored. "First of all, my people have no interest in *your* kind or the human realm. My interest in your research is singular. Secondly, if any of *my* people found out that I was working with you, doing what we're doing, then we'd know it already." He wiped the blood from his hands on a rag, after which he flung it dismissively near the corpse on the table—another failed experiment.

"How can you be certain of this?" Kheelan asked. He wondered how that bastard could be so calm in the face of his crumbling plans. He'd spent years helping Alefric rise to power, and now, with his beloved King dead, he concentrated on his own rise. He wondered if perhaps it should have been Alefric assisting *him* to power all along, and he wasn't going to let some group of animals stop him from becoming whom he now knew he was meant to be.

"My people are not subtle, Captain." Frederych looked squarely at Kheelan and said, "If they knew we were here, we'd both be dead already."

That should have given him pause, the emotionless way the other Fae talked about their destruction, but he was too far gone in his rage to worry about that. Reysken's betrayal of him would only be avenged once his spawn was wiped from all the realms. He would not stop until she and the rest of the meddling animals were dead. And then he'd make sure that all shifters knew that their place was firmly under the foot of his boot heel and nowhere else. He would also deal with that royal brat, Eyrica, once and for all. Where his King had failed he would not.

"Frederych! Gather the men. We are going through the Veil tonight, and we are going to end this once and for all. Then I will take *my* rightful place on the throne."

****

Jason felt a sense of relief to be holding onto April once again. When he'd woken up in that frozen wasteland, he thought he may never see her again. It had been torture to think that he and Donovan had left April alone to fight against Kheelan. He was still having a difficult time processing the fact that he and Donovan had actually seen and spoken to April's long deceased mother.

He'd barely even been paying attention to the rest of the people in the room, but when Gabe snarled in response to Corrine's time running short and the fact that she had mates, he felt the sharp stab of his Alpha's pain trickle down the link they shared.

"Mates?" Gabe repeated through gritted teeth. Jason could see the veins bulging in his neck and his wolf was dangerously close to the surface.

It was awful feeling this pain and confusion coming from their usually stoic leader. He wasn't the only one confused about Corrine's declaration, but Jason's thoughts were derailed when a sharp pain lanced through his chest.

"Jason! Donovan!" April cried out as they collapsed once again. Jason clutched his chest. He could feel the blood begin to drip from his nose. He tried hard not to scream out in the wake of all the pain, trying to spare April as much as he could.

"What's happening, Corrine?" April asked frantically. "I thought the spell in the tattoo healed them?"

"Damn Kheelan! Yes, the spell my sister cast brought them back to us from the Shadow Realm, but mortals were never supposed to set foot there. It has taken much of their energy from them, and the original poison is still in their system." Corrine looked from Erica to April as Ben and Leo helped Jason back onto his own cot. "April, you and Eyrica will have to work together to heal them. I think now that they are no longer being pulled into the Shadow Realm, your healing powers will work on them. Their bodies will need time to help you push out the poison, however."

April placed one hand on Jason's chest and her other on Donovan's, while Erica focused her healing powers on the bites. It felt like she was attempting to draw out the poison through the entry points while April repaired the damage already done. Jason felt something trickling from his nose again and ran the back of his hand across his nose to wipe away some of the blood, but when he looked at his hand, it was covered in some dark, inky substance instead. The pain in his chest was subsiding slightly, but he felt exhausted, his eyelids heavy.

"Poison," he heard Corrine say to his left. He hadn't even realized that he shut his eyes. "She's filtering it out of their bodies."

For the next couple of hours, he remembered drifting in and out of consciousness, April, Erica, and Corrine, vigilant at his and Donovan's side. Finally, when he heard Donovan's voice, Jason opened his eyes slowly.

"There he is. We thought you'd sleep all day, you lazy bastard." Donovan's cheeky smile was a welcome sight, but it couldn't hide the dark circles under his brother's eyes and the blatant look of exhaustion that must have mirrored his own. Jason felt like he'd been run over by a semi-trailer, but at least he felt normal beat-to-hell and not poisoned-and-dying-beat-to hell.

"He's lying of course. Donovan's only been awake for a few minutes himself." April's sweet voice was music to his ears. "How are you feeling, baby?"

"Better I think, or at least getting there," Jason replied, slowly sitting up and then swinging his legs around.

"Gods, it's good to see you both up and without the black goop leaking out of you," Gabe said as he walked into the room and strode over to a tired looking Corrine.

Just as Jason stood on shaky legs, Leo rushed into the room. The expression on his face clearly showed that he wasn't bringing good news.

"Gabe, the patrol on duty says we have company in the woods on the southern border of the property."

"Who?" Gabe asked, his facial expression quickly turning into that of a stone-cold predator.

"Fae! A group of armed Fae and they are headed straight for us."

Chapter Twenty-One

Instinctively, Jason and Donovan positioned themselves in front of April as Gabe barked out orders. She could see them struggling through their weakened state to stand tall in front of her, and she found herself facing two muscular backs this time, reminiscent of the first night she'd met Jason. She'd laugh if the current circumstance wasn't so dire.

She placed a hand on each of their backs. "Please don't ask me to sit this one out." They both turned to face her. "I won't listen anyway," she added with a weak smile.

"Defense only," Donovan said, though he looked none too pleased. "You will be nowhere near the front lines, you understand me, April?"

She nodded. The last thing she wanted to do was be responsible for making them lose focus while trying to protect her. Every part of her screamed to beg *them* to sit this one out, but they would never listen. Their duty to their pack and their overwhelming need to protect her would easily win out over her concern for them. Instead, she offered an alternative.

"You can tap into my energy. Erica explained how mates can share their life force, how they were even able to channel some of her power and feed her their strength when she was weakened."

"Will that harm you in any way?" Jason asked. He and Donovan had both turned to look at her again.

"No," she replied with confidence. Erica assured her that it was safe. They'd only be stronger together.

As they all headed outside to defend their territory and to finally put an end to Kheelan's reign of terror, Gabe filled Donovan and Jason in on the information he got out of the Fae guard they had "captured" earlier. Kheelan had obviously instructed the guard to get caught in order to infect Jason and Donovan with the poison. They had also managed to get out of him that the humans were all being held at the same location where they had kept April. The Fae scum even bragged about the fact that many of them had been experimented on and did not survive, just before the poison had consumed him and turned him into ash.

April sent up a silent prayer to the Goddess, hoping that her coworker Dee had not been one of those unfortunate experimented on victims.

A few minutes later, more wolves gathered at their side as they reached a large clearing in the forest behind Gabe's property. April could sense, however, the rest of the pack remained hidden behind and all around them in the forest.

Gabe's phone rang. "Fifty," he said after he hung up the call.

Donovan seemed surprised. "He comes into our den with only fifty men?"

But then she saw the group being led by Kheelan into the clearing. They stopped a healthy distance away and like the sea parting for Moses, they all parted for Frederych. Kheelan flashed a wicked smile in her direction as the vile Freddy got down on one knee and placed his palms flat on the ground.

It didn't take long to see why Kheelan thought he only needed fifty men.

The ground beneath her started to shake, but unlike the earthquake Erica had caused where she could have brought down her entire palace, this one was controlled. Frederych was manipulating the earth, and bending it to his will.

The Fae charged at them while Kheelan stayed to

guard Frederych. The ground remained unsteady, all but where Kheelan's men stepped. The battlefield became a mass of chaos as swords collided and the sound of flesh being torn apart resonated in her ears. She got a chance to see just how lethal Erica and Corrine were with their blades while she threw her powers from her in short bursts of energy in an effort to destabilize some of the attacking guards. Only fair to even out the playing field, she thought.

A face in the crowd stood out to her just then. The other guard she had blasted out of her way when she broke free of her captivity came charging toward her. She sent a targeted burst of power in his direction, but he sidestepped the blast and she herself fell victim to the shaking ground, landing on her back. Another guard appeared and pinned her hands above her head.

April struggled to break free of his hold as she kicked her legs out toward the one she recognized. He smiled smugly and poised his sword to strike at her chest, but then she heard her name being called.

Donovan.

The guard never had a chance to strike. His arms were ripped from his body before Donovan whirled around to catch the guard's falling sword. He ran the sword through the Fae's heart, and April watched as his body turned to ash. Her hands were freed as well after Donovan tossed the sword to Jason who was standing behind her, and he immediately decapitated the one restraining her. That Fae turned into two separate piles of ash, one for his body, and one for his head.

"Behind you," she yelled at Donovan as another Fae guard charged him. Donovan faltered slightly, and so did April from the shaking ground. She saw the sword pierce through his arm. "No," April yelled again, only, this time, she let her power out in front of her, feeding it and some of her strength to Donovan, who quickly and expertly dispatched his attacker. She turned to Jason and sent him the same energy as he battled and dismembered his own assailant.

Satisfied that she was safe for the moment, Donovan and Jason ran back into the center of the fight, but not before each of her men planted a swift kiss on her lips. When it was Donovan's turn, however, she quickly healed up his wound. She could feel their strength returning and sent them even more of her energy.

"Right," Erica began as she came up behind her and pulled her farther back from the battle and the shaky ground, to where Corrine was currently waiting for them, "It's time to end this. The three of us are going after Kheelan."

"What about Frederych? He's too powerful."

As if on cue, the Fae goon showed them all just how powerful he was when the ground began to crack open. Flames burst forth from the cracks, burning some of the wolves. It was shocking to see the range of control this mysterious Fae had upon the elements. His powers felt somehow different from anything Erica or Corrine had shown her. April heard a tortured yelp of pain. Her first instinct was to run and heal the fallen wolf, but Erica held her back. "If Kheelan dies, they'll have no one left to follow."

Erica was right, of course. They needed to sever the snake's head to ensure that this would be their final battle.

"We'll worry about Frederych when Kheelan is dead," Corrine added before she turned to look at April. "I need you to let us take care of the physical fight with Kheelan, April. You've just barely begun to wield your sword, and while I have no doubt with practice you will become a fierce warrior, Kheelan has had more than one lifetime to learn how to kill. Your powers are your greatest strength, and a smart fighter always uses their advantage. That's how you stay alive."

April hated that her aunt was right, but there was no room for pride in a war. She would attack where she could do the most damage. Both Corrine and Erica seemed to be relieved when she nodded her agreement.

The women surreptitiously backed away toward the woods. They needed an element of surprise to take Kheelan and to make sure that Frederych stayed focused on his task instead of them. She shuddered at the thought of what other surprises that Fae goon had in store for them. His abilities were even greater than she had known from her torture sessions with him.

They made their way closer and closer to where Kheelan stood guard over Frederych. April knew that it would not be easy to take him down. From what Erica had told her, he was a damn good fighter, very skilled with his blade, but she and Erica had their energy and Kheelan had not looked too well the last time she had seen him.

Just as they were about to make their move, however, April heard the sound of a twig snapping from somewhere much deeper in the forest. She still hadn't gotten used to the enhanced hearing her wolf gave her.

"Stop," she whispered, placing a hand on Corrine and Erica's shoulders to halt their movement.

"What is it?" Erica and Corrine both asked simultaneously.

"Someone's coming."

Another twig snapped, and this time Erica and Corrine heard it, too. "Damn, woman. You've got great hearing."

The three of them poised for a fight with their unseen assailant. Moments later, a very large, heavily tattooed giant of a man, stepped out from behind a tree and April saw both Erica and Corrine visibly relax.

"It's okay, child," Corrine said. "He's a friend. I'm fairly certain he let you hear his approach. His kind can be one with the forest when they need to be."

"Forgive me, Your Highness." The large man bowed. "I did not mean to startle you and your ladies. I came to help."

"Ishaya, how did you know about the battle?" Erica asked.

"I *borrowed* one of Kheelan's guards earlier. I wanted information about the one called Frederych. I inquired. He answered."

"I don't imagine that they will be getting their guard back?" Corrine shook her head and smiled at the man.

"Not in one piece, no. He was very cooperative, though. Even told me where he was headed." He inclined his head in the direction of the battlegrounds.

Though Ishaya had looked scary to her at first, upon closer inspection April could see that he had kind eyes. He smiled at her when he caught her staring at him. She couldn't look away from him, though, despite being caught, not when she noticed the strange tattoo around his eye. "It's moving," she whispered as if only to herself. "Just like the symbols on the rocks."

The sound of an explosion finally diverted her attention. The force of it nearly knocked them off their feet. Even the big guy looked off kilter for a moment.

"Now," Erica yelled over the successive booming sounds of more explosions. "He dies now."

"Frederych is mine," Ishaya stated simply as he walked past them. "He owes me a life."

Elena Kincaid, Maia Dylan, and Sarah Marsh

Chapter Twenty-Two

"He owes you a life?" Erica asked the large man who had befriended her as a child and had stood by her and her parents for many years. Most of the forest folk kept to themselves and did not interact with the Fae unless they had to, but Ishaya had always been a friend to their family, and Erica couldn't have been more grateful for it than in this moment. In all those years however, he'd never spoken about his family, and she had a feeling she was about to find out why. The sadness that shimmered in his eyes when he turned back to face her had Erica stepping forward to hug him.

Ishaya sighed and returned the hug, being careful not to squeeze too hard and hurt her. "He took my sister, Arethusa, as his Fated One, even though she did not feel the connection to him in return. When the bond is forced upon another, they can choose to accept the claim, or reject it. Arethusa rejected it, and Frederych killed her. He took a piece of my heart that day, so now I am going to take his from his chest as it still beats and show it to him before he dies."

Erica looked up at him somberly. "That sounds perfectly fair to me. A life for a life. Justice is yours to take, and we will leave Freddy to you, my friend."

"And *we* will deal with the douche-tard Kheelan," April added.

Ishaya pulled away from her and moved toward the battle, his destination clear. "I will wait for you to engage with Kheelan before striking at Frederych. Good hunting, my Fae sisters. May your blades ring true and this day bring you the vengeance you all so very much deserve." Then, with a decidedly bloodthirsty grin, Ishaya melted into the forest.

"Now there goes a man on a mission," April said

as the three of them stood for a moment and watched as Ishaya seemed to disappear before their eyes.

Corrine moved in the same direction. "And speaking of missions, we have our own. Let's go get us some of that bastard who has caused so much pain to the people we love."

"Ain't that the truth," Erica said as the three woman gathered closer together. "Time is of the essence with this one. With the kind of power they are throwing around out there, our side does not have a whole lot of time. I reckon as soon as we get near him, we hit him with as much power as we can, try to disorient him as much as possible so we can strike with our blades."

April nodded. "That sounds like a good plan. If we focus all our power at him at once, we should be able to put him on his ass long enough for you to strike."

Corrine grinned. "We go on three."

Erica nodded in agreement as she followed her *Quenya* closer to the battleground, April at their side. The fight was still raging, and the sounds of wolves and Fae locked in battle rang through the forest. As they stepped to the edge of the tree line, they crept silently into position, just behind and to the left of Kheelan. They could see Frederych kneeling on his right, his hand still buried in the earth.

Erica saw April scanning the forest around them. "Where is Ishaya?" she mouthed silently.

Erica winked and shook her head. No matter how hard April looked she wouldn't find him. Despite their size, Ishaya and his kind could never be found in a forest if they did not wish to be. They were a race of formidable warriors with talents all their own.

Corrine held her hand out, her three middle fingers aloft. *Three,* Erica thought to herself and gripped the hilt of her sword, infusing it with her energy to bring forth the blue blaze along the blade. April did the same as Corrine tucked one finger away.

Two.

Erica should have been scared, or nervous, but she felt neither emotion. She was calm and completely in control. Kheelan had been her tormentor, her jailor, and her nemesis for many years, and now he would get what he deserved. Corrine folded away another finger.

One.

Taking a final deep breath, Erica's focus narrowed on the evil bastard who stood not more than ten feet from her. She was so damn ready for this.

All three of them moved forward, Erica and Corrine taking point, when that final finger disappeared, emerging from the forest with a singular focus. Get to Kheelan, knock him on his ass, and make him bleed— preferably a lot—stab him again, and then keep going until the fucker exploded into nothing but ash.

As soon as the three of them had taken two steps from the forest, Erica let loose with a pulse of energy, forcing it out toward Kheelan. She felt April's pulse of power mirror hers from the right, and Erica grinned anticipating what was to come. Kheelan was finally going to learn never to underestimate a woman.

But nothing happened.

Erica frowned as she dug deeper, forcing a strong stream of energy toward her target. She heard April curse softly beside her and knew that she was dialing up her attack at the same time.

What in the hell is going on? With everything they were throwing at this asshole, he should have been writhing on the ground in pain. But there was nothing. She pulled the energy back into herself. Corrine looked at her and April in concern, and Erica could only shake her head. She had no idea how Kheelan was not feeling the effects of their attack until finally Kheelan turned to face them. A crazed gleam of madness shone in his eyes, and the sadistic smile on his face told Erica that he either knew that they had been there all along or he had suspected that they would come for him. But it was the sight of the shimmering tattoo around his eye that had her heart leaping into her throat. She saw it moving.

"Didn't you think I would safeguard against your powers?" Kheelan sneered.

"To be honest, no, we didn't." Erica shrugged. "Let's face it, Kheels, you aren't exactly the sharpest tool in the toolbox, if you know what I mean."

"You think to insult *me*?" Kheelan's voice was harsh. "There is nothing you can say that would affect me. But it is nice that you came together. I have all three of the Fae *whores* I hate most in this world in one place. I do also thank you all for coming to me alone. It makes it that much easier to kill you now."

Erica smiled, knowing that it would piss the bastard off. "Aww, you're most welcome, Kheels. But why in the name of the Goddess would you think that we would come alone?"

Kheelan frowned in confusion, his eyes darting to the battlefield where her men and April's were still fighting. She then followed his line of sight over to where Gabe was currently dispatching a member of Kheelan's army while flat on his back.

Turning back to her, he said, "There is no one else to fight by your side."

In that moment, almost as if the move had been timed perfectly, Ishaya seemed to appear from the ground beside Frederych, his body shedding some crazy glamor that had him blending with the earth around him. He gripped his prey by the throat.

Frederych grunted as Ishaya lifted him off the ground with his right hand clasped around his throat. He then proceeded to pound his left fist into the Fae's face, over and over again.

"What the hell is this?" Kheelan spat as he stepped towards Ishaya's direction.

Erica moved quickly to stand in his way as Corrine and April moved at the same time to surround him. "That would be Ishaya. He is a lovely man who enjoys quiet walks in the forest, a cup of whiskey at the end of a hard day's work, and spilling the blood of an enemy who has taken someone dear from him. That last one is a characteristic he and I share."

"As do we all," Corrine added, and Kheelan turned to look first at her, then spun to see April on the other side of him. When April grinned and waved her sword jauntily in his direction, Kheelan growled.

"You think just because you surround me that I am somehow at a disadvantage?" Kheelan sneered. "You are fools if you believe you will defeat me with blades."

Erica watched dispassionately as he held his large sword before him with both hands, but then somehow, the blade split in half so that he now held two identical blades, one in each hand.

"You do not have the skill to best me," Kheelan bragged as he dropped into a fighting stance—his right leg forward, both legs shoulder width apart for balance. He also looked a lot stronger than how April had described, as if he had not been stabbed by Corrine at all. The blade in his right hand was pointing directly at her, and the other he held in a reverse grip so the blade pointed behind him, ready to swing it in either direction. "Not individually or together. So come at me now and let us end this as it has always meant to end—with your blood spilling from your severed heads. You can join your damn Goddess for all I care."

"Wow," April said sarcasm clear in her tone, "have you ever thought about a career in greeting cards? That was almost poetic. And we hate to shatter your illusions. Well, that's not completely true, since I for one love the fact that we get to do that, but I digress. Where was I?"

Corrine swung her blade in a quick slice, making it ring through the air, and Kheelan spun in her direction. "You were about to tell the traitorous, narcissistic Captain that he may be underestimating our battle skills just as he's miscalculated our strengths in several situations now. How is your King, Kheelan? Dead, isn't he?" she taunted. "Oh—that was rather insensitive of me, wasn't it?"

A furious roar escaped Kheelan as Corrine's words hit home. He lunged for her with a staggering blow that brought her to one knee when she blocked it with her own blade. The fact that April came at him as well from the other side was no doubt the only reason Corrine still had her head, but dammit, that girl was supposed to be hanging back! True, now that the bastard seemed to be unaffected by their powers, they needed all the advantages they could get, but Erica just prayed it wouldn't cost April her life. Erica needed to remember that despite their taunts, Kheelan had not been exaggerating about his sword fighting skills. In fact, it appeared that he had gotten even better with his dual sword technique.

Erica lunged at him just as he aimed his sword at April, blocking what could have been a mortal blow. He managed to knock Corrine down again, separating her from her blade, but Erica, anticipating his next move, blocked his sword with hers, buying Corrine time to regroup and scramble for her lost sword. He focused on her and April meanwhile. April was able to block several blows, but Erica could see the strength with which Kheelan was swinging was wearing her down quickly. Then suddenly she stumbled and lost her balance.

Erica struck with full force, but Kheelan blocked her with his right hand and then time seemed to move in slow motion as Erica watched Kheelan's left arm come around, the sun glinting off the Fae blade as it sliced across April's chest. At the last moment, Corrine managed to get to April and grab her from behind, pulling her back, but April's cry of pain rang out as the blade still sliced through her skin. Erica sent up a thank you to the Goddess. If not for Corrine's quick intervention, the blade would have gone clean through her, and Erica would have lost yet another person she cared about to this asshole.

Fury soared through her at that thought, and she swung hard while he was distracted by the blow he'd delivered to April. Erica felt her blade move through his skin, muscle and bone. Kheelan returned the strike, and she felt the searing burn as his sword sliced her left thigh. She instinctively brought her blade straight up in front of her before lunging forward again. This time, she landed a direct hit to the side of Kheelan's face. He leapt back and Erica smiled, satisfied from the bright red trail of blood along his cheek.

Erica heard a loud cry coming from her left, one that sounded like it came before a death blow was delivered, but she did not turn in its direction. She knew that it was Frederych, succumbing to his fate at Ishaya's hands. It did, however, capture Kheelan's complete attention, because he spun to face the noise, realizing his battle advantage was now at an end.

Erica moved with all the speed and skill she possessed to strike at her enemy whilst he was distracted. She used her blade to force one of his up, while Corinne swung her blade with both hands using all of her strength to knock his other sword to the ground. Erica then plunged her own sword into his stomach up to the hilt.

She leaned in, holding his gaze. "For my parents."

Then a second blade came quickly after, driving deep through his right side. Kheelan's eyes widened in shock. Corrine leaned in and whispered, "For my sister and for my queen."

Kheelan could not hold in the pained cry as the third blade slid through his left side. This time, it was April who stepped in. "For *my* parents and for my mates."

The three blades were crossed over each other within him. They began to glow, growing brighter and brighter with each passing second. Kheelan's head fell back, and he looked up into the sky shaking his head in what Erica could only assume was denial. He shouted something in ancient Fae intermingled with cries of pain, both of which were cut short when he exploded into ash before them.

Erica turned away as the ash rained down on the ground around them. When she looked back at her friends, she grinned at the sight they must have made, their blades still crossed, all three of them wearing matching expressions of satisfaction.

"That was beautiful to watch," Ishaya murmured as he stepped closer to the three of them, "Are you ladies all right?"

Erica turned to look at him, raising an eyebrow at the amount of blood on his hands and clothes. "Just a few cuts, my friend. We'll live." The three of them finally lowered their swords, and Erica immediately placed her hand on April's chest. "Not trying to feel you up, sweetie, although these do feel quite lovely, but that *is* a nasty gash."

April shook her head and smiled at Erica. She then placed her hand on Erica's thigh, and moments later, both of their injuries had healed.

Satisfied, Erica turned back to Ishaya. "Frederych died hard, then?"

Ishaya smiled, and his face shone with an almost boyish glee. "Yes, my Queen, he did. It was a long time coming, and my dear sister's soul can rest with the Goddess now knowing she has been avenged."

Erica let out a tired chuckle as she moved to place her blade in the sheath she wore across her shoulders. "I am glad, Ishaya. Now Arethusa is avenged, and you can finally—"

Corrine gasped from behind her. "What dark magic is this?" Erica spun, drawing her sword in the same movement.

At first, Erica had expected to see some nasty resurrection of Kheelan, or somehow a trail of blood instead of ash, indicating that he somehow managed to escape as he had the last time, but all she saw was Corrine pointing at Frederych's body. His entire torso had been torn open, and true to his word, Ishaya had removed his heart. It lay there unmoving beside the man's body.

Corrine turned to look at Ishaya, her face pale and her eyes wide with shock. "He did not revert to ash in death in the human realm. How can this be? He is Fae."

"Yes, he is," Ishaya said with a shrug of his massive shoulders, "but he is Dark Fae."

Chapter Twenty-Three

"And what did Corrine say to that?" Donovan asked as he used the towel he had in his hands to gently wipe the water off his mate's soft skin. The three of them had shared a leisurely shower as soon as they'd gotten home. A shower filled with long kisses, lingering caresses and whispered words of affection.

"Well, she didn't really say much," April replied after a moment's thought. "She seemed really shocked that they still existed. Before that though, the big guy, Ishaya, had said something about being a part of the Dark Fae, and that he was bound by the same secrecy, but didn't elaborate any further. I heard him mutter something in another language that Erica had roughly translated to mean that the cat was out of the bag now. Then we heard Gabe yelling for any of Kheelan's men who were alive to come out of hiding because he was getting sick of kicking aside piles of ash and he was looking for another fight."

Jason chuckled from where he stood in the doorway to the bathroom. "Yeah, for a moment there it looked like he was reenacting that scene from that movie where Gene Kelly is kicking and playing in large puddles of water. Fucking ash was flying everywhere, and that shit hurts when you get it in your eye, and then it freaks you the fuck out when you realize it was once a person. Once the ground stopped rocking we were able to dispatch the rest pretty damn quickly."

Donovan finished up drying their mate and lifted her into his arms, following Jason out of the bathroom. "I was so proud watching you tend to our pack mates. I knew you must have been tired. Jason and I could feel your fatigue, but you and Erica didn't stop until every last one of us was healed."

April sighed as she laid her head against Donovan's shoulder and he pressed a kiss to her head. "And then you two played the part of cavemen and whisked me away and brought me home."

Donovan laid her on the bed and moved to lie down next to her as Jason mirrored his move on her opposite side. "My wolf was screaming at me to bring you here and take care of you. We felt it when that bastard's blade cut you, April. I don't think I've ever been as scared as I was in that moment. My brain knew that Erica healed your wound, but I still *feel* the shock of what happened. You could have been killed, and Jason and I were nowhere near you to protect you, fighting our own battle, unable to run to your side. I just needed to touch you for myself to make sure you were whole."

April sighed again as she snuggled against him, and Jason groaned from behind her. "And we wanted to get you naked and feel your skin against ours. Fuck, baby, it was horrible fighting those bastards and not knowing where you were, or if you were safe."

April wriggled until she was on her back, looking up at him and his brother. "I'm sorry you went through that, but I am not sorry that Erica, Corrine, and I did what needed to be done. I will *never* be sorry for being there when the monster who tortured Jason and robbed me of both my parents met his demise."

Donovan gave her a slow smile, one he knew reflected his erotic intent. "I'm not going to insist that you apologize for that. I get that you needed that. But we *are* going to punish you for keeping us in the dark about your plan to confront him without us."

April's eyes widened. "Punish me?" Her voice was slightly higher than normal, and she sounded breathless.

"In the most delicious way," Donovan promised as he slid down the bed a little and rolled onto his back, tugging her up and over him, and encouraging her to move up towards his mouth. He inhaled deeply taking the intoxicating scent of her arousal deep into his lungs. "Fuck, you smell delicious. I need to get my mouth on you. Jason's going to prepare you a little while I make you feel good, mate."

"Prepare me?" his mate asked as he settled her over him.

"Lean forward, sweetness," Jason said from behind April, "and spread those knees wide. Give Donovan something to work with, and I am sure he'll make it more than worth your while."

April smiled as she moved to comply, spreading her knees and bringing Donovan's deliciously pink treat closer to his mouth. With a groan, he gripped the firm globes of her ass in both hands and latched onto her pussy with his mouth.

"Oh, Goddess!" April squealed, pushing her knees out further and giving Donovan more access to the soft flesh he was quickly becoming addicted to. He set into a rhythm, swirling his tongue through the rapidly swelling folds of her pussy, before flicking the very tip up and over her engorged clit. He listened to the increasing sounds of pleasure she made, taking his cue from her reactions to his oral ministrations.

When she tensed slightly above him, he knew that Jason was preparing her ass to take one of them, making sure that she would feel nothing but pleasure. Whatever he was doing, their mate approved of, if the flood of hot cream that exploded in his mouth was anything to go by. With a growl, he took everything she had to give and settled his tongue over her clit. He was determined to drive her up and over the edge of sanity and into pleasure quickly.

April groaned, her body beginning to shake violently above him. "Donovan, that feels so damn good, and Jason … I never knew. It's too much. Oh, Gods, I'm gonna come!"

Donovan thrust his tongue into her pussy as it clenched and her body shook with the force of the orgasm that crashed through her. He stayed with her through the throes of her pleasure until her body slumped against him. With one last kiss to her swollen pussy, he slid out from beneath her. His heart was pounding, and his dick was harder than it had ever been before. Tonight, he and Jason would take their mate at the same time, and claim her fully. His wolf howled in approval within him.

It is about damn time!

****

Jason had stared at the glory of his mate as she came for them. By the Goddess, it had been miraculous to see her in such throes of passion for them. They had come so close to losing her today, but she was a warrior and she was a survivor just as she had always been.

"That was beautiful, baby," Jason murmured into her neck as he pulled her head down and kissed her deeply. "I can't wait to be deep inside of you when you come this time."

"Top or bottom, brother?" Donovan asked before he stole April's lips for himself.

"Mmm, bottom," he answered, lying back against the pillows on their large bed. "I want to see every feeling flashing across our mate's face as she comes for us again."

Jason grabbed his aching shaft and stroked up and down, spreading the pre-cum that emerged when April's hungry eyes followed his movements and she licked her lips. "Baby, I could come right now just from the way you are looking at me. Why don't you climb on up here and help me out with this?"

"Don't mind if I do," she answered with a sexy smile as she threw one leg over his waist and rested her sweet ass over his thighs. "Why don't you let me do that?"

Jason groaned as she replaced his hand with her own, working his cock in long, tight strokes. When she moved her hips up so that he could feel the wetness of her pussy against his balls, he lost his patience. She squeaked when he grabbed her hips and lifted her just enough.

"Put me inside of you, baby. I can't wait another second."

"Oh yes…" They both groaned as she sank down on top of him.

He looked up at his brother and knew exactly what Donovan had in mind for their delectable little mate. She was promised a punishment, and Jason's dick twitched inside of her just thinking about how she would react to what was coming. He moved her hips back and forth a fraction, just enough to give her a tease, and then he slid his hand around her neck and pulled her down for a kiss.

"Lean forward a bit more, baby," Donovan instructed as he reached over to the night table and grabbed the tube of lube. "Just try to relax."

Jason chuckled as he felt April tense up from the butt plug that Donovan had just inserted. He felt it through the thin wall that separated his cock from it. She felt even tighter around him, making Jason even more grateful that they had purchased it for her.

He tried to soothe her as he leaned forward and

took one of her nipples into his mouth, sucking and drawing on her until she finally moaned and collapsed against him.

"Good girl. We'll leave that in for a bit to stretch you while I deliver your punishment," Donovan said.

Jason had a second to see April's eyes go wide with alarm before the crack of Donovan's hand across her perfect ass rang out in the room.

She stilled above him. The second smack had her closing her eyes, and when Jason resumed sucking and biting her nipples, she let out a soft moan. Donovan continued on with the spanking, delivering slap after slap, rubbing her ass in between. When Jason looked back up at her face, her eyes were open and he could see the look of confusion on her face. At the same time, he could also feel the ripple of her muscles and the wetness around where he was buried deep inside of her.

"Oh! How can that feel so good?" she whispered. She gyrated her hips, trying to move over him, reaching for her pleasure. "I need to come … please."

"You took your punishment beautifully, baby. You deserve a reward."

Jason felt Donovan remove the plug from her ass, and they both laughed at her disappointed grunt. He knew, though, that her disappointment would be very short lived as he watched his brother add lube to himself and then some more to April's ass. It was time for all three of them to get their reward.

****

The anticipation was killing her. Jason felt rock hard inside of her and all she wanted to do was move, but they held her still. Didn't they get how much she needed the both of them as well? She'd almost lost them to Kheelan's wretched poison, and she could have lost them again in battle, though they both fought valiantly even in their weakened states. All she wanted now was to be connected to them both at the same time, to feel them with her, inside her, and all around her. That and she was horny as hell, sporting a serious case of the female equivalent of blue balls. Her newfound wolf mentally chuffed in agreement.

Donovan leaned over her back and whispered in her ear. "You can tell your wolf to pipe down now." With that, he slowly pushed inside of her, he and Jason filling her completely.

April closed her eyes as the sensation of total fullness ran through her body. There wasn't any part of her that wasn't connected to them at that moment. As Jason and Donovan began moving in sync with her sandwiched in between them, she felt herself building to what she was sure would be an earth-shattering orgasm. Sparks of desire streaked through her entire body, finally settling in her lower belly.

When she opened her eyes again, Jason was staring at her with what she could only describe as pure love and adoration. He cupped her breasts and moved forward to suck on her nipples. Donovan held onto her hips, driving their movements, while he sporadically landed kisses to her shoulder blades and the back of her neck.

"You feel so good around my cock, angel," he whispered in her ear again. "Gods, you're amazing."

"Mmm, and she tastes so fucking delicious," Jason added. "I'll never get enough of these sweet berries or her honey-flavored cream."

"Ugh," she groaned successively. Their words only drove her desire further as they pushed in and pulled almost all the way out alternatively. She thought she would physically combust when they began to move even faster.

"Feels good, baby?" Jason asked when his mouth was free of her nipples.

"So good! I want to come so badly. Please…" She was at the brink now as they hit spots inside of her she didn't even know she had. She stood at the edge of a cliff, waiting for that final push, and then finally, gloriously, it came when Jason pushed up deep inside of her and held still, just as Donovan did the same on his end.

She collapsed on top of Jason, her ass still in the air, and she fisted the sheets on either side of his head while crying out her release, over and over again. Spasm after spasm ripped through her as Jason and Donovan both spilled inside of her. Their loud panting breaths and moans filled the otherwise silent room until all three had exhausted themselves completely.

April could barely breathe, let alone move after how her orgasm ravaged her body. Donovan pulled out first and collapsed on his stomach beside her still on top of Jason. Jason lifted her hips slightly and pulled out as well. He wrapped his arms around her as if to hold her in place, but she had no plans of moving off of him just yet anyway. Especially after Donovan threw his arm over her and she had that feeling of being completely connected to both her men again. And none of them it seemed could form a single word.

She had no idea that any time had passed when she opened up her eyes. As a matter of fact, she could not recall shutting them in the first place. It turned out that they had all fallen asleep right where they lay for a good two hours. The sky had turned dark in the interim, and she had no desire to get out of bed until the next morning … or perhaps afternoon … or perhaps what she and her mates needed was to spend the week shut in to catch up for all of their lost time. In any case, that was something for tomorrow to figure out. As Jason and Donovan quickly cleaned her and themselves up with some wet washcloths, all she wanted to do was close her eyes again and fall asleep snuggled in between them.

"I love you both so much," she told them when they crawled back into bed. Donovan threw the covers over them.

"I think I loved you from the moment I sensed you sniffing my back," Jason said with a chuckle. He pressed his lips against her cheek and held them there for a moment.

"I can't even tell you when it was I first knew," Donovan began. "There was so much chaos and turmoil going on before I ever even got to meet you, that when I finally held you in my arms between those bars in your cell, I already knew that I loved you."

Donovan placed a soft sweet kiss on her lips, and her eyes welled up with tears from their declarations. As she lay there safely in their arms, she had so many things to be thankful for. For starters, her mother and father for sacrificing themselves to protect her, her mother's foresight that not only saved her again, but saved her mates as well, and for her own intuition, that pull she'd felt to pick up and move to Vancouver where Jason and Donovan filled the gaping void inside of her and stole her heart.

Her fate had been decided long before she had ever even met them.

Epilogue

Unfortunately, April didn't get the week's rest and time she so desperately craved with Donovan and Jason right after the battle. In fact, that first week had been a grueling one. After Donovan and Jason had whisked her away, Gabe had gone back to the cliff with some of the pack in an effort to rescue the remaining abducted humans. Ishaya had accompanied him in order to open the gate to the Veil after Gabe insisted that Corrine remain at the pack house to get some rest.

Kheelan, or Frederych rather, had added some kind of block to that particular portion of the Veil, preventing entry. By the next day, after several more failed attempts to enter made by Ishaya and some of his kind, Gabe had no choice but to let Corrine, and then Erica assist, as well as some of the most powerful Fae magic practitioners that had been in residence at the palace. It took three days for them to finally break through, and in the meantime, April, who insisted on being present, couldn't help but feel helpless due to her lack of knowledge of the Fae world. She was also sick with worry at what they would find when they managed to get inside. She knew for a fact that not all of the humans survived and sent up daily prayers to the Goddess that Dee was all right.

What they found inside was horrific, to say the least. Thirty-six humans in total had been kidnapped over the course of six months, both men and women, even though Kheelan had known that the child of Reysken and Ilyra had been a female. Frederych had needed both sexes to experiment on, for whatever purpose still remained unclear, but over half of them were found dead, discarded like trash in a pile in one of the cells. Beakers filled with different colored liquids were haphazardly placed all around the room, some of them nearly empty. The bloodied bodies had been mutilated, distorted, in ways April could not have ever imagined, traces of the liquids staining their skin. One particular male had his insides turned out, exactly like what she felt Frederych had tried to do to her. She fled the room, thankful that at least Dee wasn't among the pile, and vomited in the hallway.

"Let's take you home, baby. You shouldn't have to see this," Jason had said while Donovan rubbed her back."

"No," she had croaked when she finally stopped throwing up. "I need to be here. I need to find Dee. It was my fault she was taken in the first place, and besides, they'll need my help with the healing."

"No, it wasn't your fault, angel. I will not allow you to take the blame for this." Donovan was adamant.

The remaining humans were located shortly after. Some were a little worse for wear, malnourished and dehydrated like April's coworker Dee, and some were in fairly bad shape. April rushed over to her as soon as she found her, but the glazed look in Dee's eyes tormented her with guilt.

What she must have seen. April may have grown up in the human world, but something deep inside of her had always screamed that she wasn't like the rest of them. Perhaps that's why it had been so easy for her to accept the existence of wolf shifters when she first stumbled upon one and the rest of the supernatural world when she had learned about it later. For Dee and the other abducted humans who had survived, however, the experience must have seemed like the stuff of fairytales and horror movies. The human brain isn't always capable of processing that which logic deems impossible—

sometimes it simply breaks.

The Fae magic practitioners administered a serum to the humans once April had healed what she could, one that was coupled with a hypnotic suggestion. They altered their memories to coincide with the cover that had been created—the victims had fallen prey to a serial killer.

Gabe had shifter friends in the police department and in the coroner's office, therefore, the actual details were easy to cover up and all of the mutilated bodies were burned, otherwise there would have been no logical explanation for what had actually been done to them. Frederych, since he still had a body, was made to be the culprit. An elaborate human back story had been created to show means and motive, a falsified location, and a grainy photo of him was released to the press. The final touch was his demise, creating a scenario of how a few heroic humans managed their escape and took down their captor.

April had also been added to the count of missing humans to explain her prolonged absence, though technically, she had been in fact been kidnapped by Frederych. She decided against returning to work now that her true purpose for relocating had been revealed to her, and instead, she was offered a position at the medical clinic located right off of Gabe's property, one which treated shifter kind.

Two weeks after the battle, when the news stories about a crazed serial killer had started to die down, April felt as if she could finally relax into her new life. Dee was doing well. April had called to check on her almost daily after the rescue, but eventually, Dee had stopped taking her calls. Not that they had ever been close, given the short time they had known each other and the fact that April had kept her and everyone else she worked with a distance, but April had thought that perhaps even though Dee's memory was altered, something in her gut still made her steer clear of all things supernatural.

April had finally managed to spend some quality time with her mates after that first week. They continued to take her mind, body, and soul to new sexual heights, especially when Donovan and Jason learned to tap into the phantom energy she had first discovered in the bathtub with Jason. Donovan had even managed to turn the tables on her one night, binding her arms and legs with her own blue energy, immobilizing her as she did him, and she loved every minute of it. She loved the two of them even more with each passing day.

She also got to bond more with Erica and Corrine. She knew her aunt wanted to get closer to her, but April also knew that she was another excuse for her to avoid Gabe. She and Erica didn't press her to talk about it, though. They knew Corrine was in love with Gabe, but knowing that she had two mates explained why she never got together with Gabe. April's heart ached for her. She wanted Corrine to have exactly what she had with Jason and Donovan, her Fated Ones.

April and Erica were sitting with Corrine in the den, reminiscing about her parents and Erica's childhood when Gabe appeared in the doorway. He obstinately stayed there unmoving, preventing not only Corrine from escaping a conversation with him again, but trapping her and Erica in a very awkward situation.

"I think it's time we finally had a talk, Corrine."

"There's that rotten word again," Corrine said matter-of-factly while turning to face the window instead of Gabe. "Time! There's not enough of it. I need more of it."

"What the hell does that even mean?" he snapped.

"I have loved you for so many years." His voice cracked on a pained note.

April looked at Erica, wishing that somehow they could escape in order to give Corrine and Gabe their private moment, but Gabe kept talking, his voice strangled. He probably felt like he had no choice but to say what he needed to right here and now since Corrine kept avoiding him. April had never seen the Alpha look so vulnerable.

"I don't regret a single moment of loving you, even knowing you are meant for someone else. I couldn't have helped it even if I *did know* when we first met. You had plenty of *time* to tell me."

Corrine's voice was thick with emotion when she whispered, "It's complicat—"

"Complicated?" Gabe cut her off, raising his voice enough to make Corrine turn to finally look at him. April saw that her expression mirrored Gabe's pained look. "You owed me the truth no matter how complicated it was." His voice finally softened. There was no way he could miss the pain written on Corrine's face.

"You're right," she said in a defeated tone after a moment's pause.

Corrine looked as if she was about to say more, but a commotion at the front door diverted all of their attention.

"Where is she?" April heard a masculine voice yell from the hallway.

Seconds later, what April could only describe as a chiseled blond sun-god with golden eyes, came barging into the den, pushing right past Gabe.

"Braxas? What the hell are you doing here?" Gabe asked.

Corrine's face paled as the sun-god called Braxas centered his gaze on her.

"We've been friends for a very long time, Gabe," Braxas said, still looking only at Corrine. "We've had each other's backs more times than I can count, which is why I left after the battle in the Fae realm." Braxas then finally turned to look at Gabe. "Out of respect for you both, I stepped away, despite how much it made my heart break to know my mate was in love with another man."

"*Your* mate?" Gabe's expression was a mixture of sadness and fury.

They both turned to look at Corrine as Braxas continued. "I saw her, and I knew. Almost immediately after, we were fighting a battle. I felt the stab Kheelan delivered to her as if he had stabbed me, but then I also heard you cry out in pain, Gabe. She was then healed and the two of you were locked in an embrace, the love you had for each other evident. It would have been better if I had actually been stabbed in that moment and less painful, I can assure you."

"Is this true, Corrine?" Gabe asked. "Is he your mate?"

Corrine said nothing, but her lack of response must have said everything to Gabe. He shut his eyes and curled his hands into tight fists at his sides. April could see his knuckles whiten.

"You should leave … now," Gabe whispered through gritted teeth, his eyes still shut. April wasn't sure if he was talking to Braxas or Corrine, or even if he meant for them both to leave until he finally opened his eyes and looked directly at Braxas, his wolf very close to the surface. "Out of respect for our friendship, don't make me ask you again, Braxas."

Corrine stood up from the couch looking horrified at the scene playing out before her. "Stop it." Her words came out as a whisper. "Stop it," she repeated several times, each time her tone growing firmer, but her plea fell on deaf ears, especially since the two men were now growling loudly at one another, locked in a staring contest.

Braxas sounded more animal than human when he stated, "I am not leaving without her. Never again! She is my mate. We. Are. Bound."

Just when April thought that things would finally quiet down around here, more chaos ensued as their beasts erupted from the skin of both men. The sound of fabric ripping, snarls and gnashing teeth, echoed in her ears.

The End

Elena Kincaid, Maia Dylan, and Sarah Marsh

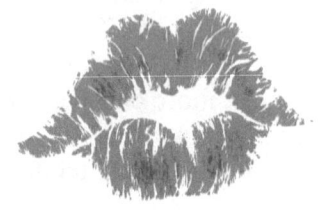

EVERNIGHT PUBLISHING ®

www.evernightpublishing.com